SENTINEL
City of Destiny

SENTINEL
City of Destiny

LANDEL BILBREY

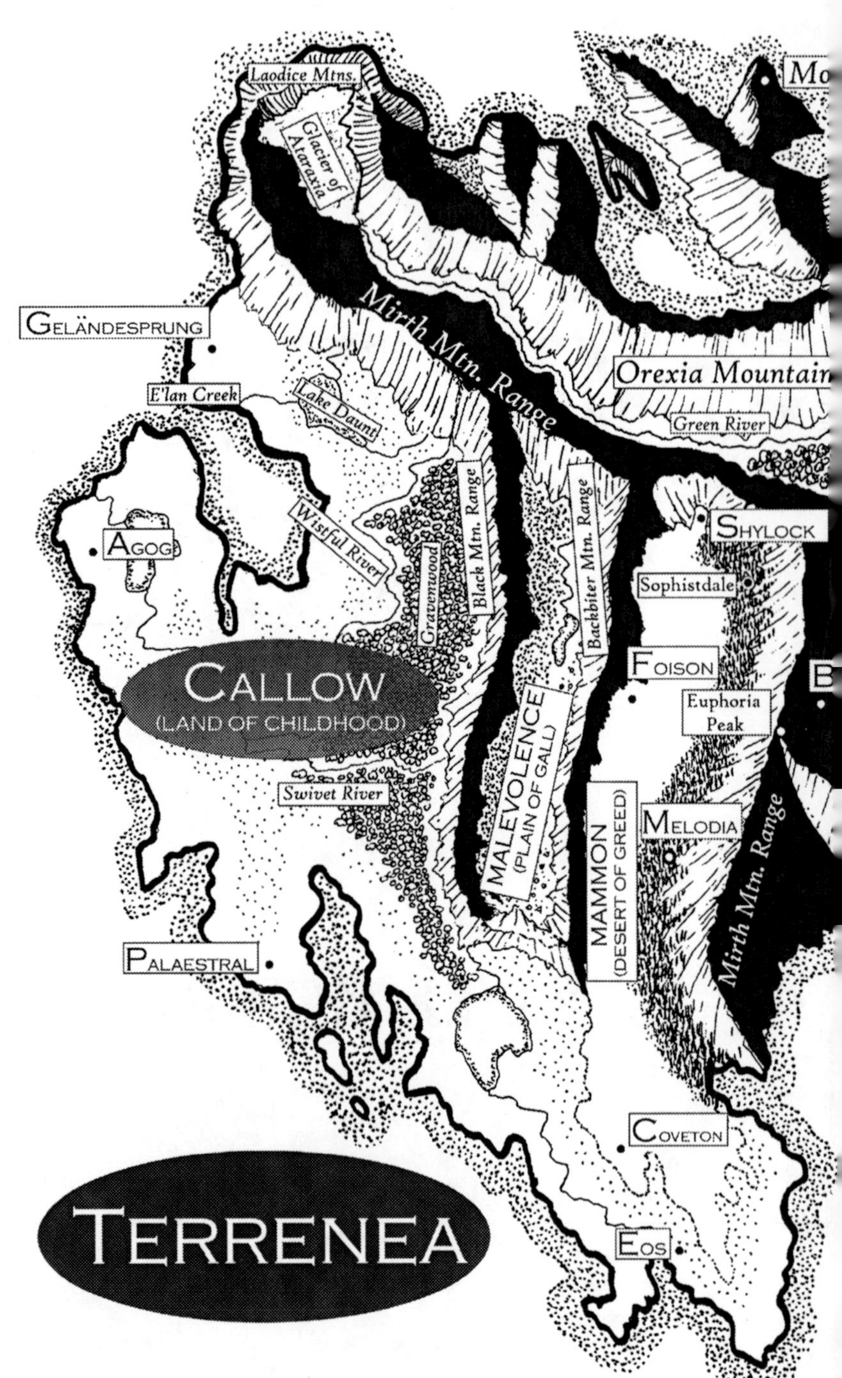
Laodice Mtns.
Glacier of Ataraxia
Mirth Mtn. Range
Orexia Mountain
Green River
Geländesprung
E'lan Creek
Lake Daunt
Wistful River
Gravenwood
Black Mtn. Range
Backbiter Mtn. Range
Shylock
Sophistdale
Agog
Callow
(Land of Childhood)
Foison
Euphoria Peak
Malevolence
(Plain of Gall)
Swivet River
Mammon
(Desert of Greed)
Melodia
Mirth Mtn. Range
Palaestral
Coveton
Eos
Terrenea

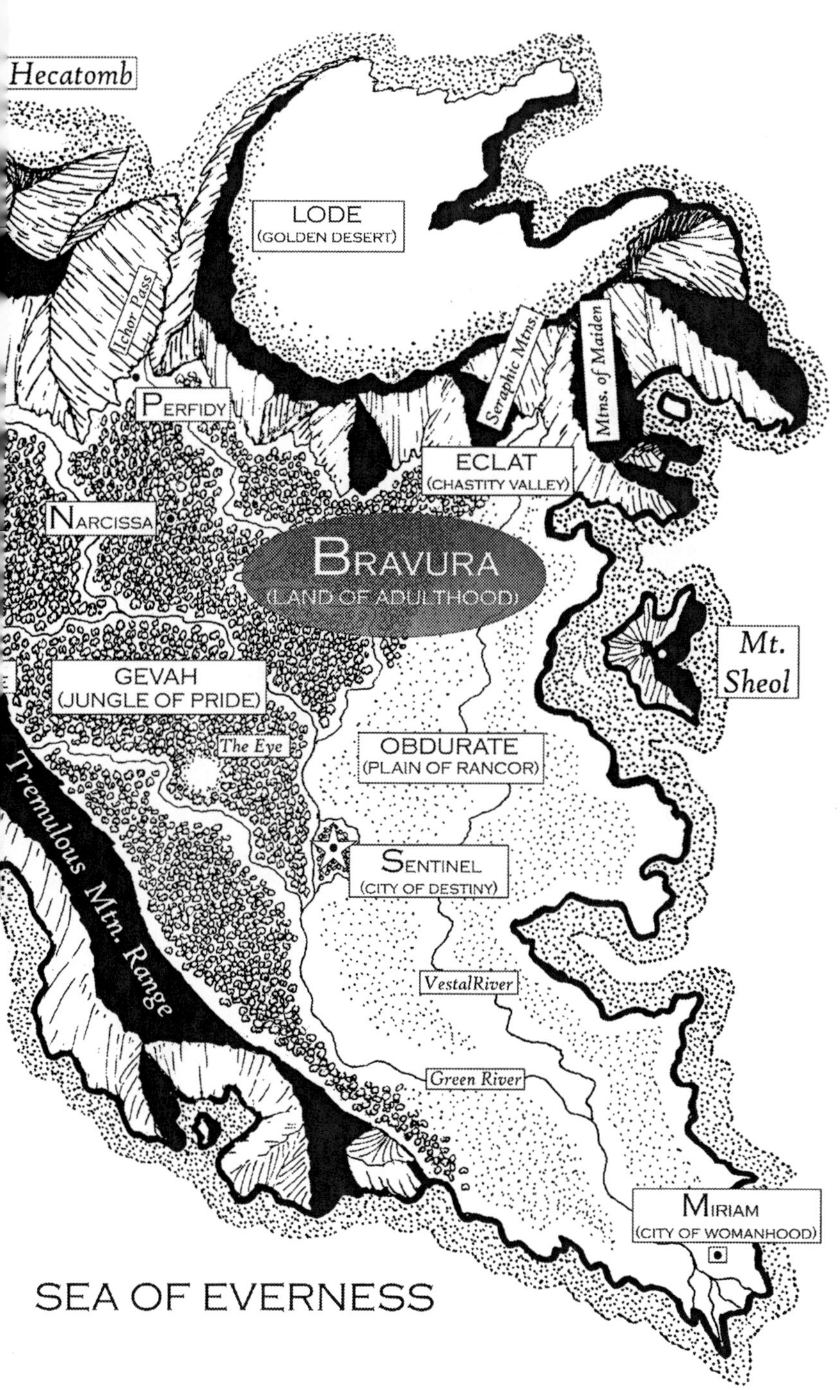
Hecatomb
LODE
(GOLDEN DESERT)
Ichor Pass
Seraphic Mtns.
Mtns. of Maiden
PERFIDY
ECLAT
(CHASTITY VALLEY)
NARCISSA
BRAVURA
(LAND OF ADULTHOOD)
Mt.
Sheol
GEVAH
(JUNGLE OF PRIDE)
The Eye
OBDURATE
(PLAIN OF RANCOR)
Tremulous Mtn. Range
SENTINEL
(CITY OF DESTINY)
VestalRiver
Green River
MIRIAM
(CITY OF WOMANHOOD)
SEA OF EVERNESS

Published by Bridgemaker Books

Illustration reference photograph of fallen knight used by permission.
Photographer Thomas Goskar, www.pastthinking.com
Illustration reference photograph of flying eagle used by permission.
Photographer Richard Ambler
Illustration reference photograph of large goose used by permission.
Jack Deo

Cover and Book Design by Bill Kersey

Bilbrey, Landel.
Sentinel : city of destiny / written and illustrated by Landel Bilbrey.
p. ; cm.
ISBN-13: 978-0-9793744-0-1
ISBN-10: 0-9793744-0-5
Audience: ages 8 and up.
SUMMARY: Allegorical tale of Jerol and Jadan, twin brothers, who travel from Callow, the land of childhood, to the city of Sentinel searching for the four keys of Mettle. Sentinel is the city of true manhood. During their quest, evil Azrael and his many minions challenge them at every turn. Includes glossary of terms and devotional guide.
[1. Fantasy--Juvenile fiction. 2. Conduct of life--Juvenile literature.
3. Moral education--Juvenile literature. 4. Ethics-- Juvenile literature.
5. Brothers-- Juvenile fiction. 6. Siblings-- Juvenile fiction.
7. Christian education of young people-- Juvenile literature.
8. Christian fiction.] I. Bilbrey, Landel. II. Title.
PZ7.B553 S46 2007
[FIC]--dc22 2007902487

Printed in the United States of America

May 2007

For my sons,
Hudson and Clark

"Hear, my son,
and receive my sayings,
And the years of your life will be many.
I have taught you in the way of wisdom;
I have led you in right paths…
Take firm hold of instruction, do not let go;
Keep her, for she is your life…
… the path of the just is like the shining sun,
that shines ever brighter unto the perfect day.
The way of the wicked is like darkness;
they do not know what makes them stumble…
Keep your heart with all diligence,
For out of it spring the issues of life.
Put away from you a deceitful mouth,
And put perverse lips far from you.
Let your eyes look straight ahead,
And your eyelids look right before you.
Ponder the path of your feet,
And let all your ways be established.
Do not turn to the right or the left;
Remove your foot from evil."

Solomon, King of Israel 970-930 BC

CONTENTS

Table of Weights and Measures

One Hand = Three Inches
One Thumb = One Inch
One Step or Pace = Three Feet
Stones Throw = One Hundred Feet
One Full Moon = One Month
One Season = Three Months
One Day = Twenty-Four Hours
One Summer = One Year
One Sack of Corn = One Hundred Pounds

Seasons of Time

Season of Birth = Spring
Season of Warmth = Summer
Season of Change = Fall
Season of Ice = Winter

A Note to Parents, Teachers and Caregivers

Growing up is easy. Growing up to be a man of good character is hard.

How do boys learn what it means to "be a man"? Is it genetic? Is it intuitive? Does it just happen? Boys through time have learned what the definition of manhood is from observing and listening to the men living around them and the culture of their day.

If the behavior of men around them in words, deeds, and actions shows God's love, then there is a greater probability that they will grow into men who will live their lives showing God's love. Conversely, if the behavior of men around them displays the world's perspective, there is a greater likelihood they will grow into men who will approach life with a worldly perspective.

Every moment boys are watching us. How do we deal with life's challenges? Are we being proactive in showing them the way to manhood? Are we diligent in showing them how God's Word instructs us to live? Are we leading them with purpose or just letting life happen? They are learning every day from someone or something - A father, a mother, a brother, a television character, a commercial, a billboard, or a song.

I encourage you to read Sentinel to or with the boys in your life. Use the story as a springboard for sharing with them your life's lessons. Let it offer opportunities for you to be hands-on in explaining your understanding of how their Creator wants them to live. Have conversations with them about how they can become godly men—men of courage, integrity, service, and vision.

A few suggestions for using *Sentinel* as a teaching tool:

- A parent, teacher, or care-giver could explore the meaning of the asterisked words found in the glossary while reading to a boy or group of boys.
- A parent, teacher, or care-giver could read to a boy or boys and use the questions in the back of the book to explore the story's deeper lessons. See the "Reflections of the Blade" section.
- For older boys, a parent, teacher, or care-giver could invest in the boy's future by assigning and paying the boy to read the book and then produce a book report by answering the questions in the back of the book. See the "Reflections of the Blade" section.

The world of today and tomorrow needs godly men. How will our boys know unless we tell them?

Preface

As my sons were approaching middle school, I began to think about the countless temptations and challenges they where about to face as teenagers. The adolescent years are when God's enemies lay the most traps. Split second decisions made in the heat of the moment affect young hearts for a lifetime. So, equipping my sons early in life to avoid making bad choices became an important goal. Would they be ready? Had I done everything I could do to prepare them? Had I given them the tools for good decision-making? More important, had I opened the instruction manual provided by the Maker of their souls—God's Word? Had I shown them His warning labels for their safety?

I could see that their surroundings were slowly coloring their world. Like sunglasses, popular culture was affecting the way in which they viewed their reality. Much of what they saw through the world's glasses was not truth. And not knowing the truth usually brings bad choices that lead to bad consequences.

Sentinel was born out of my desire to fit them with a pair of "Son-glasses," glasses through which they could see the truth. My hope was to identify and communicate to them foundational character traits that God wants to see in a mature man. I wanted to help them see the target they should aim for with their lives. Courage, integrity, service, and vision are the values I have identified as the target. If they will aim their words, thoughts, and actions at these four standards, the likelihood of a successful life is greatly increased.

You may have other values that you believe are equally or more important. My ultimate hope is that Sentinel brings to you and your boys not what I think, but that the story opens up your life to what God wants. Thank you for taking time to explore *Sentinel, City of Destiny.*

It should be noted that, throughout the text, Biblical scriptures are drawn upon. These scriptures are allegorically referred to as the *Logos.* References to the Logos teachings are my paraphrases taken from several versions of the Bible; they refer to Biblical verses. To find specific, supporting scriptures the following code can be used: Logos 20:22:6 would refer to Proverbs 22:6 (the twentieth book of the Bible, beginning with Genesis, the twenty-second chapter and the sixth verse).

Also, Christian baptism is referred to allegorically as Gerhorsam (vow of submission) in the story. Please note that the point I am seeking to make is that having a submissive, obedient heart toward God is what marks a true man. The emphasis is about character not salvation. Without true submission to God, a man is a man in name only and not in character.

Many place, event, and character names have meaning. To glean a full understanding of the story's message, a glossary has been provided in the back of this book. Words that have meanings that may be found in the glossary are indicated by an asterisk (*).

Finally, all views, opinions, and interpretations expressed in this book are solely those of the author and are not necessarily shared by any of those acknowledged for their support, the book cover designer or the book's interior designer.

Acknowledgements

I thank the following friends for their help, advice and encouragement during the development of this project:

First, Brent Baldwin and Dr. David Faulks.

Next, Pastor Matt Brewer, Pastor & Dr. Jim Chatham, Chad Collier, Mason Cordell, Michael Cronic, Jeff Deason, Pastor Dave Deerman, Rusty Faulks, Leslie Hudson, Ray Mullican, Butch Simmons and Andrew Wilson.

A special thank you to the editor, Heidi Weimer and the book cover and interior designer, Bill Kersey.

And an extra special thanks to my wife Carolyn, whose inner beauty is an inspiration to me, my sons Hudson and Clark, who teach me daily about my relationship with my heavenly father, my dad, Willie H. and my mom, Verdina, who are living examples of integrity and service, and my sister, Gelia who has shown me the meaning of courage.

Chapter 1

The Offering

"Again, he led Paladin to a very high mountain and showed him all the kingdoms of the world and their splendor. 'All this I will give you,' he said, 'if you will serve me.'" Logos 40:4:8

It was the Season of Change. The firefan trees were morphing into a puzzle of reds and yellows. Towering high above the shorter trees stood rows of majestic tabors keeping watch like faithful soldiers over the peaceful forest below. The giant old trees made Jerol feel like an ant in the grass. Fortunately, down on the ground, the trail was not as overgrown as those he had traveled since leaving his hometown of Gelandesprung.

Layers of leaves had piled up during many Seasons of Change carpeting the way. The moist, spongy mulch made a welcomed cushion for each step. Traveling here would be much easier.

Jerol followed the forest maze until walking out into a wide clearing. Across the gap stood a tall, ivy-covered wall. He could hardly believe his eyes! The grand, old

Wall of Devoir stood guarding the object of his quest—Sentinel, the ancient city of destiny. Soon he would be welcomed as a brother into manhood's hallowed court. Dusk had arrived and he needed to find his way to the other side before nightfall.

Jerol would need to mind his steps, for the Enemy was ruthless and had placed many trap doors along the wall. He was determined not to fall for the adversary's cunning tricks. He leaned back and with his eyes began searching the weatherworn wall, looking for clues to where the single, true gate might be hidden.

The wall's surface was uneven and coarse, draped with dark green ivy and a strange, web-like moss. Spreading out to his left and right, a wide strip of clearing lay between the tree line and the wall. Jerol turned to his left and headed north where the wall traversed up, and along the edge of a rugged cliff.

The darkness of night was steadily descending like a heavy curtain. There was no moon, and seeing was becoming increasingly difficult. Nonetheless, he followed the wall's perimeter up hill until coming to a narrow brook gently flowing from underneath the wall's foundation and near the top of the incline. The rippling stream ran down a gentle slope and then off the cliff in an arch of spray. Jerol decided to bed down for the night just outside the base of the wall. The only light was being provided by a large swarm of curious fire moths.

"Looks like a good place to make camp," Jerol thought. So, he sat down to rest and began to stare at the flickering reflection of the friendly moths in a small pool of water about three steps downstream from the wall. "What an interesting place," he told himself. "I hope my brother is already safe behind the wall. Mother and Father will be so proud of us. I can hardly wait to see what the city will be like."

All of a sudden, a loud racket moving rapidly through the underbrush and somewhere beyond the cliff's dark edge brought Jerol at once to his feet. He watched with concern as treetops, illuminated from below, violently shook from side to side. A strange light was moving at a furious pace directly to him. A radiant, glowing creature eventually emerged from the adjoining brush about sixty steps behind him to the south. The creature stood erect, dwarfing the trees beneath it. Its beauty was unlike anything he had ever seen before, and its unusual light lit the surrounding wall and countryside like a thousand blazing lamps.

The creature stood studying Jerol's bulging eyes and then began to speak with a pleasing voice. "Jerol, do not be afraid. I mean you no harm. I am Candor*, seraph of truth! I have heard of your great bravery and want you to lead my army. I am willing to offer you anything your heart desires. Just say the word, and I will make it so. I wish to be your friend." He moved closer, and then paused. "I have also come to warn you; you have not been told the truth. Do not desire to sit on the King's court, for if you do, you can expect only misery and suffering. Come, stay with me." The angel's smooth face looked serene and inviting. "Do you really believe the King's promise of blessings? What does an old King know about a young boy like you? If he truly cares about you, then why does he allow you to suffer? Why would he make you struggle for so long to find this place?" The creature paused, leaning toward the tiny boy. "I know why. It is not hard to understand. The truth is, he really doesn't care about you. He only cares about pushing you around for his amusement. Listen— today is a new day. If you will follow me, I promise to make you commander over my most seasoned warriors! Your foot will no longer have to touch the battlefield. Instead, you can send your warriors to fight in your place."

Jerol stood speechless and confused. Prayer, who was circling and watching from high overhead, began screeching, wildly flapping his wings. The commotion snapped Jerol back to his senses.

"Whom should I believe?" he pondered. The angel's generous offer had stirred doubt deep in his soul. "The journey has been hard. If the King were so loving, why did he allow me to suffer so much?" Jerol queried. "And ruling over an entire army would be a once in a lifetime opportunity." He was feeling confused. The stranger seemed sincere enough. But still Jerol's heart was telling him to be cautious. He searched within his soul for guidance from the Scrolls. "For the hallowed sword is quick and powerful, piercing even to the dividing of soul and spirit, joints and marrow, and is a discerner of the thoughts and intents of the heart." (Logos 58:4:12) "That's it!" he thought.

Keeping his eyes transfixed on the creature, Jerol drew his weapon and slowly brought it into view. He eased the blade above his head with its flat side turned toward the seraph. The sword's metallic surface began to throw and magnify the angel's brilliant light. One light beam, then another, and yet another, until the area was saturated with a light even brighter than that of the creature!

Blinded by the light and stirring up a great cloud of dust, Candor quickly turned his head away and began slowly moving closer to Jerol. The cautious boy kept his eyes focused and moved with the approaching form keeping his sword between them. The brave boy blinked and squinted, struggling not to lose his bearings through the rapid flashes of blinding light and swirling dust.

As the light was reflected from the sword and onto the enormous seraph*, a bizarre and distinct shadow appeared behind him upon the cloud. To Jerol's astonishment, its outline did not coincide with the shape of the lovely creature standing before him. Instead, he saw the shadow of an enormous dragon! Instantly, the creature's disguise was foiled.

"I know who you are!" Jerol shouted, moving back and pointing his sword in the dragon's direction. "You are the leader of the Shadow World!"

Realizing that Jerol could no longer be deceived, the blazing imposter dropped his clever disguise and transformed into its true self, mirroring the shadow in the distance. His face was long and grotesque with a mouth lined with long sharp spikes for teeth and a forked tongue as long as Jerol was tall. His body was a mass of muscles and sinew encased in a suit of scorched, rough, leathery skin. A thick putrid stench began to fill the air. Inexplicably, light seemed to be absorbed into the beast's enormous body. The countryside behind the monster began to turn pitch black.

The dragon threw back its head and howled with a hideous laugh that shook the jungle. "Little boy! You will never enter Sentinel! You are nothing more than a frightened little bug and certainly no match for me. I am Azrael, the immortal ruler of The Damned. I have been since the beginning. Just one flick of my finger can destroy thousands of your puny kind! What makes you think you will ever become a warrior, when you are still afraid of the dark? Run back home to your mother before it's too late, little boy!"

And with that, the demon pointed a disgusting finger

at Jerol, and then shouted into the woods, "Get him!" Jerol turned, wondering to whom Azrael was speaking. Sin had broken from the bushes near the wall and about thirty steps to his right, and was running at full speed straight at him! The devilish swine was mad and grunting with his head down low to the ground. Drool was dripping from his twisted mouth. Jerol watched in wonder as the beast began morphing into some other kind of creature with each step he took. He reared up; lifting his front legs from the ground and began running on his hind legs. His front hooves transformed into hands with long fingers and sharp claws. Jagged bat-like wings flexed and pulled free from his gristly back. Two bright red lights glowed from where his eyes used to be.

As Sin began whipping his wings, a bolt of black lightning shot into an old, dead tree to the left of Jerol. A shower of invisible sparks and smoking wood exploded out at the startled boy. Jerol raised his shield just in time to deflect the fragments. He could not see the sparks, but he felt their heat across his skin. Jerol readied his sword for action while he watched Azrael out of the corner of his eye.

When Sin got to within about twenty steps of Jerol, he was suddenly squashed to the ground! Prayer had been flying guard in the clouds and decided to intervene. The great bird had folded his mighty wings and fallen straight down, like a boulder, onto the back of the unsuspecting beast! Jerol reeled backward as the two titans tumbled on the ground. Screeching, Prayer clawed and grabbed between Sin's rubbery wings. Sin started screaming back, exposing sharp tusks, and throwing his head from side to side trying desperately to stab Prayer's chest.

After a couple of near misses, Prayer released the kicking fiend and bolted upward. Sin jumped to his feet, opened his mouth, and began spewing out pieces of flaming brimstone into the sky. The super-heated rocks riddled into the great bird, stopping him in midair. The blows were hard, forcing him back down to the ground. Sin pounced, lunging at his nemesis, but once again the agile bird dodged and catapulted straight up and in a blur, disappearing into the darkness of the night. The angry demon frantically searched the sky in every direction, but he could not see the bird anywhere. Then, BOOM! Prayer suddenly reappeared from the shadows and delivered a decisive blow to the back of Sin's head. The stunned animal's ugly face dug hard into the dirt. Prayer held on tightly to the bunched-up skin folds on the back of Sin's neck, this time lifting him off the ground and high above the trees. The demon became so irate that he began to spit fire. He punched at the air with his powerful wings and legs, trying to break free, but his resistance was no use; Prayer was not letting go. Under great protest from Azrael, Prayer carried the screaming imp through the sky and out of sight.

The battle was over in a matter of moments. Jerol wasted no time in moving back to face Azrael, whose beady, red, glowing eyes were growing brighter. The ancient dragon began pacing from side to side. Jerol could hear his prehistoric bones crack with each step. Words from the Scrolls began to fill the boy's thoughts. "Believe and not doubt, because he who doubts is like a wave of the sea, blown and tossed by the wind. Be self-controlled and alert. Your enemy prowls around like a roaring lion looking for someone to devour. Resist him, standing firm in the Logos, because you know that your brothers throughout the world are undergoing the same kind of sufferings. After you have suffered a little while, you will be restored and made strong, firm and steadfast. Resist him, and he will flee" (Logos 59:1:6; 59:4:7; 60:5:8,9,10).

The cursing giant moved closer to him but then stopped, standing only steps away. Azrael quickly leaned forward, extended his neck and stretched opened his massive mouth. Instantly, jets of scalding steam exploded out from somewhere deep inside the demon. The air began to fill with a loud roar, like a large whirlwind, as blue hot flames and molten brimstone, heavier than lead, began spewing out at Jerol!

The Dark Lord knew that he had one last hope for eliminating the boy. So, he unleashed his entire arsenal of wickedness. Fire blew out in waves of every conceivable evil. This particular day Jerol had dressed in full armor. So, the young warrior crouched down behind his badly tattered shield and, with his right foot planted back, braced for the worst. Countless fragments of burning rock began riddling into him, jarring Jerol until he was numb. Even though the molten rock was capable of melting diamonds, somehow the tattered shield was able to deflect its searing heat! The air became thick with the smell of sulfur. If not for his faithful shield, Jerol would be consumed. The barrage of evil persisted for what seemed like days. When the assault had ended, all that was left of the demon's display of hate was a pile of smoldering ashes and glowing embers. The onslaught had pounded Jerol down and onto his back. He was banged up and bruised, yet much alive. The fearless boy sprang back up and onto his feet.

In disgust the old dragon lifted his arms, grabbed at the sky and belched out another ear-bursting shriek! Jerol knew that the only thing left for Azrael to try was to seize him with his bare hands and rip him to shreds. While the Dark Lord stood distracted, Jerol saw an opening, a chance to prevail. Throwing down his glowing shield, he seized his sword, lifted the weapon behind his head and began running at Azrael as fast as he could. But just before coming to within striking range, his right foot snagged a root on the path. He grabbed at the air trying frantically to stop his fall but was thrown hard to the ground. He felt something smash against his head, and then everything went black.

Chapter 2

Bull's Eye

"Plan carefully and you will have plenty; if you act too quickly, you will never be satisfied." Logos 20:21:5

To this day I get chills when I think of how Jerol must have felt standing alone before Azrael*. I remember too well how I felt, as a young boy, backed into a corner so far that the only thing I could see was the demon's twisted face. Just like Jerol, I had almost made my way into Sentinel when the Enemy appeared and stood to oppose me. He threatened to destroy everything I had worked so hard to get. Only by the grace of good King Deus* am I still here today. Beware, my friend, for sooner or later the Old Dragon will come looking for you, and, if you want to sit at the King's table, you had better be ready.

That is why I want to tell you the rest of the story about Jerol and his brother's perilous quests for Sentinel*, the City of Destiny. My hope is that you will learn from their experiences and avoid much trouble. Please pay close attention to their tale. I promise you that if you heed its timeless message, great shall be your reward.

My name is Lector*. I am a follower of the Light, and I live with my sweet wife, Charity*, in the world of Terrenea . Our land is a diverse and beautiful place, which rises up from the Sea of Everness. In our world, there are only two Kingdoms: the Kingdom of Light and the Kingdom of Shadows. We are blessed with twin sons, Jadan and Jerol. This is a story about their journey through the land of Callow* to the city of Sentinel. Sentinel lies in the heart of Bravura* and is the hallowed city where the revered Blades of Mettle* reside. The Court of Mettle is made up of an elite fighting force that stands watch over our great land. They are sworn to fight to the death in defense of our great ruler and his Kingdom.

According to our King, becoming a Blade should be the goal of every boy. To have the Mark of the Blade is to sit in the highest place of honor. However, to get this great esteem each boy must earn his place. First, he must traverse the open plains of Callow, pass through the mysterious Gravenwood forest, overcome the barren Plain of Gall, endure the punishing heat of Mammon, climb the mountains of Mirth, and conquer the jungle of Gevah. Most importantly, he must find the four keys to Mettle. All this he must do before he can enter Sentinel. The challenge is known as "The Crossing" and is an ancient mission dating back to the beginning of our history.

As you read this tale, you will quickly discover that, even though they are identical twins, Jadan and Jerol do not act alike. Rarely will they choose to do anything in the same manner as each other. Perhaps I can best explain their different methods with a short story from their past.

Once every summer in the Kingdom of Light, the Terrenean elders hold a special celebration called the Festival of Glister. The event is a time of thanksgiving, planning, and fellowship for all. Every Terrenean family gathers for the exciting event, and folks of every age participate. Nobody is left out. There is always an abundance of food, singing, dancing, and games for all ages. Of the many children's games enjoyed during the festival, the boys' favorite is Bull's Eye. In the game a life-sized image of a black bull is painted on a brightly colored sack and suspended between two trees. Directly behind the sack stands a heaping mound of red clay piled up from the ground to the top of the sack. Each boy brings a bow and two arrows. The object of the sport is simple. The boy whose arrow is planted closest to the bull's eye is the winner.

The winner of the contest is awarded a bull that will supply his family with a bountiful quantity of precious meat. A side of beef was highly prized; meat would provide the luxury of plentiful eating during the usually harsh and fast-approaching Season of Ice.

To play the game each boy stands with his back next to the target. Then, at a signal given by the chief elder, the boy steps fifty paces straight away from the sack. Boys between six and eighteen summers of age participate in the same match. Because of the difference between the size of the older and younger boys' steps, the elders deem this fair. Their reasoning is that the smaller contestants will be closer to the target and the taller boys will be farther away. (I must admit, however, boys who are older yet shorter walk away with the prize more often than boys in other groups!)

Well, several summers ago many boys arrived to participate in the event. Excitement filled the air as a crowd of family and friends gathered to support their much-loved archers.

Jadan took his turn by quickly stepping off his paces, spinning around, and delivering his first shot. He almost always releases his arrow before squarely facing his target. His first shot hit just above the bull's front shoulder. The result was a decent shot, but I had seen him do better before.

Each boy is given two shots so that they can adjust their second arrow from the performance of the first. Jadan quickly reloaded and without hesitation released his second and final arrow. He spent little time studying his first shot. This pattern is typical of Jadan, for his usual way to deal with tasks or decisions is to rely on his impulses. "Don't study too hard," he frequently warns.

The second shaft landed just below the bull's lower jaw. Yet again, his effort produced a fairly decent shot, but still about five hands away from the eye. Even though each shot had been respectable by anyone's standards, Jadan expressed great disappointment and stomped off the field in frustration. The crowd offered up a meager round of applause.

Next, seven other boys took their turns. One of the younger lads placed an arrow in one of the beast's ears, only two hands widths from the bull's eye! The shot was a good one and would be tough to beat.

Jerol watched the other boys as they each took their turns. He studied them closely, watching for techniques that he could use during his turn.

Finally, Jerol's name was called. He had practiced intently every day since the last contest. He had even made his bow and arrows! This time he was determined to win the prize for us.

The elder gave Jerol the signal to begin. Jerol stepped off fifty paces and then slowly rotated and faced the target. He studied the bull's eye for a few moments, then slowly lifted his bow and straightened it. He drew a slow, steady breath and pulled back the arrow's shaft against the right corner of his mouth. After a brief pause, he began slowly exhaling, and then, at the right moment, he released the arrow! The arrow found its mark in an instant. The vibrating shaft had landed about halfway between the bull's eye and its nose! The try was a good shot, but not good enough! The earshot that the younger boy had made earlier remained the closest to the eye! Jerol remained focused. He still had one last opportunity to win the prize.

He studied his first try and drew another deep breath. Then he slowly pulled the arrow up to his eye, again made a final adjustment, exhaled, and then let go! This time the hand-carved arrow pierced the sack, sinking halfway into the rubbery clay behind it. A puff of dust billowed out from the front of the sack as ripples bounced through the cloth from corner to corner.

From where Jerol stood, he was having difficulty seeing where his arrow had landed, but he knew his effort had been a fine shot. The crowd hushed as an elder moved in to get a closer look. He walked to the front of the target and leaned in to examine the arrow. Every eye focused on the old man as he turned to face Jerol. The elder then raised his hand, signaling "Bull's eye—dead center!"

The audience erupted with applause and loud cheers! Not one of the remaining boys even came close! Jerol's practice had paid off. Because of his dedication and hard work, our family enjoyed a season of excellent eating.

Several qualities in Jerol's character separate him from Jadan: his discipline of preparation, his consistency in doing his best in every situation, and his determination to make the most of his second chances. Jerol almost always plans ahead, and he considers the consequences before making a decision. He values counsel from others, including his mother and me. This method to living serves him well in everything he does.

Ever since Jadan was a little boy, however, he has had trouble following instructions. He typically ignores my discipline and continues to go his way. His stubborn unwillingness to listen to others is what gets him into the most trouble. He rarely plans ahead and usually acts before considering the consequences. These differences have always been evident, but they seem to have become more obvious during our time in Gelandesprung.

Even the manners in which the twins packed for the Crossing were different! Jerol placed his belongings in order and used a detailed checklist. He wanted to make sure that he did not leave anything out. But Jadan just randomly threw items into his pack. From every appearance, there was no forethought to his behavior.

As you will see, the dissimilarity between Jadan and Jerol will play a decisive role in the outcome of this story. So, pay attention and learn.

Chapter 3

The Gift

"The King so loved Terrenea that he gave his one and only Son, so that every soul who believes in the Prince shall not die, but will live forever." Logos 43:3:16

Despite the brothers' glaring differences, they each would still have to reach three objectives before being allowed to sit on the court of Mettle. No exceptions would be made, for these are required for all who want to make their Crossing:

1. First, each boy must receive a mysterious gift offered by Prince Paladin*, King Deus'* son.
2. Second, each boy must take part in Gerhorsam*, a ceremony where the boy must make a vow of submission.
3. And third, every boy is required to find four magical* keys. These keys will unlock the door which passes through the Wall of Devoir*and offers access to Sentinel.

To add even more difficulty to their journey, countless enemies stand in opposition to the King of Light and his followers. To this day, they are part of The Nether World, a place where the followers of evil live. Azrael*, the deceiver, rules over it. Because he can never be as powerful as King Deus, Azrael despises the King and all Terreneans.

In fact, the Evil Lord's daily goal is to hurt as many of us as possible. He especially delights in misleading and gradually turning those of us who are weak against our King. Because of Azrael's treachery, Mankind was cursed. And a special "gift" was required to restore what was lost. Through ages past Azrael has confused and diverted many boys during their difficult journey to Sentinel. Because of his hateful tricks, these unfortunate souls will never become Blades and, instead, will spend their entire lives aimlessly wandering through Bravura. In the end, Azrael and his followers will be the ones who Jerol and Jadan will have to overcome if they ever hope to become part of the King's court of honor.

Receiving "the gift" is the most important of the three objectives of a boy's Crossing. Knowing the history of the gift is fascinating and needed to understanding its role in the quest. To have the gift means life. To not have the gift in the end means death. Every boy should know the story of "the gift."

Many, many summers ago, my people came to live

in Terrenea. They were vagabonds living in a world between fire and ice, totally dependent on water for their survival. Compared to most other creatures, they were frail. Because of this, they tended to avoid natural extremes. Most were driven by a longing desire for comfort. They were mostly lovers of pleasure, sometimes even at the expense of their well-being.

However, despite their many weaknesses, the King still loved them deeply and supplied their every daily need. He gave them food and safety from harm.

In the beginning, he built for them a perfect place in which to live called Shalom*. A beautiful and spacious garden entirely surrounded and protected by four tall walls. Each wall was a well-built barrier, the likes of which they had never seen before. Long before the Terreneans' arrival, the King had constructed the walls out of tenets*, special building blocks made of a tough and magical material. They were so sturdy that nothing had ever been known to break them.

Right from the start, King Deus told the people, "If you will stay within these walls and obey my instructions for living, I will supply everything you need! But beware," he warned, "if you decide to go outside the walls and go your own way, you will surely die!"

Well, soon Azrael became consumed by Lord Deus' deep love for the Terreneans, for the history between him and the King goes way back before the beginning of time.

Ages ago, the evil leader and his army had been banished from the Kingdom of Light for trying to overthrow Lord Deus. Consequently, Azrael's every breath and thought became driven by a passion for revenge. Fueled by his rage at the good King's love and promise to provide for his people, Azrael developed a plan he hoped would trick the naïve inhabitants of Shalom.

To carry out his plan, Azrael disguised himself as a cute, approachable Corkscrew, a weasel-like creature that lived in the garden. Masquerading as this innocent-looking animal, the deceiver approached the unsuspecting Terreneans and began to enact his plot.

"Why would a loving King threaten you?" he squeaked. "Why would he tell you that if you went outside the walls that you would die? Surely you misunderstood him. The King doesn't want you to go outside the walls because, if you do, you will know as much as he knows. He wants you to stay inside so that he can have control over you. I wonder what's so important out there that He doesn't want you to know about?"

With just one innocent-sounding question, Azrael had drilled seeds of distrust into the peoples' minds. The seeds soon grew into a dangerous decision of defiance, and the curious crowd marched to the tenet gate.

Eager to see what was on the other side, they pushed open the heavy barrier. Just as the King had warned, when they walked through and beyond the safety of the garden's walls, a chain of events started that changed my people's way of life forever!

Directly above the towering door sat a tiny ancient vase. Solid black and dull, for ages past the little urn had set undisturbed. How it got there was a mystery. The motion of the gate jarred the vase, which in turn began to teeter back and forth with increasing frequency. The small clay pot worked its way from the edge and tumbled down to the hard ground below.

The brittle container shattered upon impact, exploding in a grey mass of swirling shadows and vapors. The cloud began moving as though it were a living thing. The smoke-like haze remained low to the ground then divided and began spreading out in every direction like a mass of slithering serpents. The prideful Terreneans had unknowingly released the poison of iniquity! Iniquity* was so vile that, sooner or later, it destroyed everything it touched! Iniquity would slowly invade and take up residence in all living things. If left unchecked the evil poison would eventually snuff out all life.

Sometimes iniquity can kill in an instant, but usually the toxin takes many summers before claiming victory. Today iniquity still lives, being passed on from generation to generation. The most disturbing fact about this hideous poison is not that it can destroy all physical life, but that it can entangle and slay the spirit as well!

Iniquity is by far the most destructive force known to my people. Before long the dire affects of iniquity's poison seeped into the life's blood of every living thing in Terrenea!

Despite Deus' love, the Terreneans had chosen to break his heart. As a consequence of their waywardness, they were cast out of Shalom and into a drastically different world—a world where they would have to work hard just to survive! They would have to stay alert, for without the wall's protection, Azrael's desire for the peoples' destruction would be a daily threat.

"How could they be so arrogant and disregard my love?" cried the King. "I tried to warn them! I gave them everything they needed—their food, their clothes, and a place to live! And now, because they followed their self-centered desires instead of my way, they have become infected and so weakened by iniquity that we must live worlds apart!" The King was heartbroken and began to weep.

Even though deeply hurt by the their disobedience, Deus quickly came up with a plan for the traitors' rescue! Long before Terrenea's birth, he knew that someday the people would rebel. So, he had already prepared a plan for their future salvation. The solution would be the most amazing expression yet of his love for them. However, their freedom would come at a high personal cost. Paladin, Deus' only son would do all the work.

One day as the King and Paladin were strolling through Shalom, the father began to share with his son his rescue plan. "As you know, my son, Terrenea is in much trouble."

"Yes, Father. I know," responded the Prince. "I'm so sorry that they have hurt you, and it grieves me as well that they are in such misery. There must be something we can do."

"Well, there is a way we can help them. In fact, there is only one way. But it will call for a level of sacrifice that will be hard for them to understand. Their condition is so bad that the only way they will be able to survive is through carrying out the Act of Vicar*."

Paladin stopped as the King walked on. "But, Father," Paladin exclaimed. "No one here has ever had to do that before! Its cost would be so great, trading a Royal's life for theirs!"

King Deus stopped and peered deeply into his son's eyes. "Yes, I know. But it is the only way to guarantee their freedom and restore our fellowship."

Paladin and his father knew that the Act of Vicar demanded for someone of Royal lineage to substitute his blood for the infected blood of Mankind. Because iniquity was so potent, eliminating the curse would call for the death of the Royal and every cleansing drop of his precious blood! Even though the Royal people possessed mystifying powers of regeneration and life, the pain and suffering of death would still be a heavy burden to bear.

Paladin deeply loved the King and the Terrenean people. His heart was heavy and he wanted to do something to restore his father's joy. The good prince studied what his father had said for many days. Then one day he approached the throne. Paladin stopped and faced his father. "Yes my son." Greeted the King. "Father, let *me* go and save them," Paladin solemnly offered.

The King was not surprised by his son's request, for the prince was one of a kind. King Deus could see that Paladin's mind was made up, so he agreed and the plan was set. The courageous prince would endure pain and death and be the peoples' only hope.

Though anxious to go, the brave prince would have to refrain until the time was right. So, he patiently waited for the King's command to go to Terrenea. Once given the instruction to go, he would have to go alone. Buying Mankind's liberty would call for the greatest submission of all time: going from the splendor of living with the King to living in the Terreneans' harsh world. Paladin's sacrifice would be a gift of matchless worth!

After several summers of waiting, the King gave Paladin the orders to go. The prince wasted no time and traveled to Terrenea where he lived side by side with the people. For thirty summers he lived as they lived before beginning the first phase of his mission. He began by reminding the people of their rocky past and desperate need for healing. From the start, he told them that he was King Deus' son and had come to save them.

But to his dismay, most found his story too hard to believe. As far back as the people could recall, no member of the Royal family had ever lived among them. "No Royal family would dare mingle with us," they grumbled.

It was common knowledge that ever since iniquity's release, to stand next to royalty meant one's instant death. If Paladin were really royalty, how could they be near him and survive? They did not understand. Terrenea's fall had happened so long ago that most of them were unaware that they were even sick. Since, to the untrained eye, there were no obvious outward signs of illness, most of them just refused to believe that they even needed help.

From their perspective, life was good, and all of the talk about sickness and dying was depressing and uncomfortable. Avoiding the topic altogether seemed best. Once again, Mankind's desire for comfort had clouded the truth!

Paladin refused to give up and every day continued to share his news of hope. "Listen, my friends. I have come to rescue you from the curse! I bring you a gift—the only thing that can stop the advance of this blight! Once you have it, your spirits will be freed from death, and, just as your ancestors of long ago, you once again will be able to walk beside my father! But, listen! Even though the gift will block the poison's ultimate victory over you, you must know that, as long as you live in Terrenea, you will still have to battle with its effects every day! To stay strong and overcome, you need to spend time each day with my father. Heeding his guidance will allow you to stand against Azrael's trickery. So, pay attention, my friends. Without daily help from the King," he warned, "you will be defenseless and alone! But once you are back in good standing with my father, his full resources will be on hand to help you! I am the King's only son and as such have the authority to tell you these things and to offer myself on your behalf!"

The voice of a skeptic rang out from the silent crowd. "But how can just one person offer the cure for so many?"

Looking up and into the sky, Paladin responded, "Just as all darkness, which fills the nighttime sky, flees from the flickering light of one star, so will your disease run away from the awesome power of just one drop of my blood."

The noise of the crowd began to build. The prince looked down into the eyes of the people and proclaimed, "Unfortunately, Azrael, the leader of The Damned, knows of my presence here. I know he seeks my death and soon he will stir up a crowd by accusing me with lies, and I will be brutally attacked by his followers!"

Paladin pointed to the grey outline of a distant hill. "Azrael plans to have me executed on top of Mount Hecatomb*! There I will allow my blood to be emptied on the ground to release healing for all who will believe! And when these things happen, don't be afraid. For my death is part of the King's plan for your rescue! Do not be deceived; they will not take my life from me. Instead, I have chosen to surrender it on your behalf. And remember this: no matter how cruel and hateful Azrael's blows to me may seem, the victory of my sacrifice will finally erase their sting! The release of my blood will fill all time and space with its healing power. It will never fade away! And from that glorious day forward, its power will not only be there for you, but for your children and every future generation as well!"

Pausing for a moment, the passionate Prince looked back and forth through the crowd. His countenance changed from that of a warrior ready for battle to one of a shepherd stretched out on the bank of a raging river, reaching out his staff to a helpless lamb struggling with the current. "My friends, before you can get healing from my sacrifice, you must do one very important thing. It will be simple, yet will mean the difference between your life and death."

The entire crowd grew still and leaned in toward him. "Only those of you who place your trust in my gift's ability to save you will be able to have its cure! Its healing will only be possible for those who believe that it is real!" He began to shake his head. "My father and I will not waste my suffering on anyone who does not believe us, on anybody who thinks that we are liars. Those of you who have my gift will live forever and be able to talk directly to my father as often as you choose! Those who reject my gift will continue to live bound in iniquity's grip. Those of you who reject me already have your fate decided. You will in the end be captured by Azrael and die."

Paladin's words soon proved true. The Prince allowed an angry mob to take and then brutally murder him. For two days his crushed and lifeless body lay in a small damp cave. The Terreneans were in chaos. Some were convinced that the Prince's murder proved that he had never been of royal blood. Others were confused and afraid, unsure of what to think.

Meanwhile, Azrael, giddy and proud of his apparent victory, threw a huge party for the Nether World. He was even so brash in broadcasting a prediction that without the King's help, Terrenea was doomed to self-destruction. The old demon knew that Paladin was the Terrenean's only hope. Drunk with hate, Azrael felt sure that the war of the ages was about to end, and at last he would rule over the great King of light and all of his followers.

For two chaotic days after Paladin's murder, there was a shroud of gloom and a chill that settled over the land. Some spoke of seeing a thin, black cover of clouds seep in from the North during the execution. Others claimed that they had seen the sun stop shining as though someone had put out its flame! The dark leader was beginning to get what he had always dreamed of. The people of Terrenea were starting to panic. Their hope seemed to be gone.

Just as Azrael had prophesied, the war of the ages *was* over, but its outcome was not as he had hoped. Because before dawn on the third day following his murder, Paladin* took a full breath and sat up! He had revived as if awakened from a restful sleep. With one breath, the warrior prince melted the chains of death as if they were made of wax! Miraculously, his badly broken body was totally healed and even better than before! The sun burst through and scattered the gloomy clouds, and the Prince quietly walked out into the daylight. He was showing Mankind that they could be free! All that the people needed to do was to receive his gift and trust what he had done on their behalf. If they did this, they would be given a brand new life. Afterwards, Paladin stayed with the community a short time to explain what had happened. Then he went back home to be with his father. Lord Deus' part of the plan was complete. The Terreneans now had an important choice to make.

Reeling from shock at the living, breathing proof that Paladin had offered Mankind, Azrael began spreading lies throughout Callow and Bravura. "It was just a clever magician's trick," he shouted. "He wasn't really dead. Besides, how can blood change anything? Seeing is not believing; haven't you all been fooled more than once by a mirage? Where is this hero anyway? All this talk about sickness and cures is pure fantasy! You don't feel sick, do you?" Amazingly, there were many who bought into Azrael's lies and did not believe in Paladin's promise, even after living with him, witnessing his death, and seeing him alive again!

Azrael was convincing and his influence was great in discrediting the worth of what the Prince had done. Thus, to document his son's victory for future generations, the King compiled Paladin's account into a group of sixty-six stories known as "The Logos*." The sacred writings were a collection of ancient history, poetry, law, prophecy, and much more, personally dictated by the King. Written down by Terrenean scribes and preserved on two scrolls. The Logos was not only to be the banner of the marvelous news about "the gift,"—"The King so loved Terrenea that he gave his one and only Son, so that every soul who believes in the Prince shall not die, but will live forever" (Logos 43:3:16), but the knowledge was to be used as the guidebook for Mankind's daily living—"useful for teaching, rebuking, correcting and training" (Logos 55:3:16) After completing the Logos, the King commanded that the elders of all future generations be responsible for sharing the good news of the gift with their children and fellow Terreneans.

Now you know why the gift is so important. Without it, a boy will never be able to sit on manhood's hallowed court, for no one can stand against Azrael in his own power. However, with the gift a boy has access to all of the King's wealth. If he chooses to use those resources, the gift means life and success to the Blade. To not have the gift or to ignore its power means eventual death.

CHAPTER 4

Sin and Prayer

"Don't take chances, but send Prayer often with notes to the King." LOGOS 50:4:6

"Paladin told them, this is the truth. Whoever spends time with Sin is the slave of Sin." LOGOS 43:8:34

Receiving the gift, submitting to the King, and finding the keys are critical steps that must be taken before entering Sentinel. However, there is one other important decision that Deus strongly encourages each boy to make. It is the choice of a companion to keep him company during the lonely times on the journey (and there are many). Choosing the right partner greatly increases a boy's likelihood of receiving the Mark of the Blade.

Jadan had owned four pets, but the one he adored the most was a naughty pig named Sin. Sin* was grey as ash and weighed as much as three full sacks of freshly cut corn. He was every bit of three steps long from nose to tail and six hands tall at the shoulder. One ear bent double over a pale white eye and flopped up and down when he walked; the other ear was stiff and pointed straight up. Four hook-like horns jutted from the sides of his head, and large menacing tusks filled his mouth. His hide was knobby and rough (when it was not matted in mud or covered with dirt). Sin was born with an unusually straight tail that was twice as long as other pigs'. He loved to flip his hairy whip from side to side as he strutted about.

His stare could be unnerving, for his eyes were odd in appearance. One eye stayed bloodshot most of the time and looked to be solid red. However, despite Sin's frightening appearance, Jadan was fond of him, for he had raised Sin from a piglet.

At first Jadan did not spend much time with Sin, but the more they hung around one another, the more attached Jadan became. They were almost inseparable. From the start, the mischievous little pig got into things he shouldn't. Jadan was constantly in some kind of trouble for not keeping Sin under control. Sin would follow Jadan everywhere, and greatly annoyed everyone, that is except for Jadan. Even though Sin was sure to cause trouble, Jadan just would not leave him behind. So, he chose Sin as his pal for the quest.

Jerol's choice of a partner was interesting as well. While living in Palaestral, Jerol had found a baby, Royal falcon stuck in a big patch of hook briars on the outskirts of a straw grass field behind our home. Despite its tiny size, the baby bird had no fear and was gentle. The cap of its head was as black as coal. His eyes were piercing blue, looking out from a ring of purest white. The tops of his wings were thick and dark brown and underlain by a fan of even sturdier feathers. His chest was a lighter brown

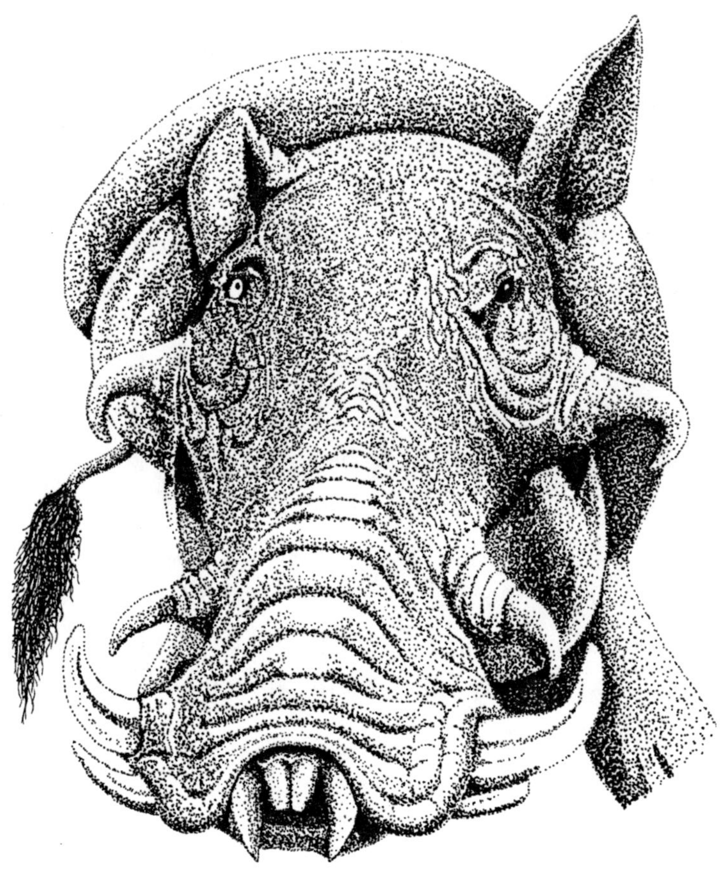

and full of muscles larger than those found on ordinary falcons. Even as a tiny chick, his talons were sharp and surprisingly powerful. Not long after he brought the baby bird home, Jerol realized just how special the little fellow was.

Jerol named his new friend Prayer*. Over the span of several summers, they became close companions. By the time Jerol was ready for the Crossing, Prayer had grown into a bird of great size. He was majestic, beautiful, and possessed enormous strength. Because of Jerol's love and care, Prayer had grown to be one of the strongest falcons in all of Callow. His wingspan had grown to be more than sixty hands wide from wingtip to wingtip! On a few occasions, while playing with Jerol, Prayer had lifted him off the ground and carried him for short distances, amazing Jerol's friends! Choosing a traveling buddy proved to be a simple task for Jerol. He would take Prayer, for Prayer had already shown to be a trusted ally.

Well, you know from where Jadan and Jerol have come. You know that even though they are twins, they have different personalities, and you have met their friends Sin and Prayer. Come; join the eager brothers as they go on the adventure of a lifetime. It's time for their Crossing to begin!

Chapter 5

Gehorsam

"Travel on the narrow path. For wide and broad is the road that leads to trouble, and many travel on it, but small is the trail and narrow the path that leads to Sentinel, and only a few find it." Logos 40:7:13

Gelandesprung, the Callow city of adventure. All Terreneans decide in Gelandesprung whether they will pursue the Mark of the Blade or settle for a less than fulfilling destiny. The time had come for Jadan and Jerol to launch out from the well-known city in search of Sentinel's keys. They had each been looking forward to their Crossings ever since they were little boys. So, when the time came for them to start packing, they could hardly contain their joy. They hurriedly packed clothes and personal belongings, were fitted for armor, polished their swords, and cloaks that Charity had lovingly made for each of them to take on their Crossing. Finally, they wrapped and added their sacred Scrolls. Packing for the trip usually took several days, but for the eager brothers, the job was done in half the time.

Every boy whose parents belong to the Kingdom of Light is given a copy of the Scrolls, known as the Logos, before leaving Gelandesprung. But the decision is left for each boy to make whether to take the sacred teachings. So, it was welcomed news when we learned that the boys had taken our advice and chosen to carry the Scrolls on their Crossing. We knew that the Logos would prove its worth once they were alone on the road, for the trip would be long and not only test their physical strength, but in time would test the depths of their souls.

At last the time to leave Gelandesprung had arrived. The impatient brothers were packed and ready to embark on their quests. Each of them had received Paladin's gift, and each had made their choice of traveling comrades. Every preparation had been made except for their vows of submission.

Submission is recognized by King Deus as another needed step in receiving an invitation to the King's table. The Logos is clear: "Go and make followers of all people, requiring their submission in the name of the King and of Paladin" (Logos 40:28:19). Submission is mandatory, the second of the Crossing's three main objectives. Boys who want to receive the full rewards of the Mark must follow through with the expectations of Gerhorsam*. Accepting the gift always comes first. Then, with a pure heart, submission should always follow.

The rite of Gehorsam is a symbolic announcement to Terrenea of each boy's devotion to Deus and His Kingdom and a visible expression of his sincerity in making the Crossing. The Logos encourages each boy to set his sights toward Mettle instead of wandering through Adulthood with no clear purpose. "When I was a child, I talked like a child, I thought like a child, I reasoned like a child. When I became a man, I put childish ways behind me" (Logos 46:13:11).

The picture of Gehorsam would illustrate each boy's willingness to turn his back on his old ways to devote his full attention to pursuing the Kingdom. His actions would show his desire to lay aside childish things to attain maturity.

The ceremony was not complicated or dangerous (as long as you could hold your breath). Each boy would make his vow and, witnessed by the town's people, be dunked under water in a pool and then lifted back up.

Always wanting to impress, Jadan was the first to announce his desire for the rite of Gehorsam. "Mother, I wish to make my submission to the King, for I know that it is my destiny to serve him."

So, arrangements were made and, a few days later, his mother, Jerol and I watched with the town's people and rejoiced as he was immersed and blessed by the village cleric. To most folks, Jadan's conduct appeared good on the outside. However, as we found out later, and to our dismay, his compliance was nothing but a staged performance by a clever actor. Jadan had only gone along because he wanted approval, not because he was expressing dedication to the King! Jadan had no intention of heeding the Logos' guidance, for he had a bad habit of ignoring its teachings. For him, success was about impressing others, not about pleasing the King.

As for Jerol, he had long been studying the cost of his decision before making his vow. He was obedient, because he was determined to serve the King no matter what the cost.

Finally, the prerequisites were in place and the time had come to leave the safety of the city; it was time to meet the challenge of the Crossing, find the four keys, unlock the door, and enter Sentinel.

It would take at least four full moons to get to their first stop. So, early in the morning, they hoisted their bulging backpacks, received final blessings from their mother and me, and bounced out to the village gate. "I am proud of you!" I shouted, as their mother waved goodbye, hoping the boys would not see her tear-filled eyes. And, with mixed emotions, excitement, and a sense of wonder, their adventure into the unknown began.

At first the boys laughed, sang songs, and talked as they passed through the golden prairies of Callow. Sin kept busy running through the brush while Prayer flew faithful watch overhead. But after a few days, the journey began to grow more burdensome. At times they struggled with boredom. The territory was new to them, and they began to feel homesick. Even so, they pushed eastward across the gentle waters of Élan* Creek to the craggy ridges of the Black Mountains. They had been told that the odds were good for finding one of the keys on the mountain's side.

After several more days of travel past a foggy Lake Daunt* and across the rolling hills of Childhood, the weary brothers stood just west of the Wistful* River. Its current was slow and the water was surprisingly clean for a channel of its size. Its crystal waters sparkled, reflecting the rich blue of the cloudless sky. Looking to the east, over the timberline of a vast forest, they could see the mountains in the distance. Its ominous ridge looked like enormous jagged teeth jutting up and into the sky. But the brothers had come too far to turn back now. Despite the mountain's menacing appearance, the boys sensed adventure and hiked on with a renewed spirit of curiosity.

Chapter 6

Gravenwood

"You shall not make to yourselves any graven image, or any likeness of anything that is in the heavens above, or that is in Terrenea beneath, or that is in the water under the ground. You shall not bow yourself down to them, nor serve them. For I Deus your King am a jealous King." Logos 2:20:4,5

After crossing the shallow waters of the Wistful River, the only thing standing between the brothers and the mountains was the sprawling Gravenwood forest. A gorgeous stand of old timber, Gravenwood stretched from the Mirth Mountains to the north and south to the Swivet River. The tall tree trunks were three steps across with stocky limbs like strong arms stretching out on every side. From the ground, the first limbs did not appear until about halfway up their massive trunks. The foliage was mostly on the ends of the limbs, so from ground level one could see all the way up the mighty trunks to their tops. The upper canopy was thick, making Jerol's job of keeping up with Prayer most difficult. Nonetheless, he knew that even if he could not see Prayer, his trusted friend would not be far away should Jerol need him. Sin stayed close to the brothers exploring the rich ground cover for grub.

To get their bearings, the brothers knelt down and removed five fist-sized, green stones from their packs. These were enchanted stones passed down to the boys from their grandfathers. Our family has used them for generations to help us find our way. The translucent stones possess a peculiar ability to attract metal. As was customary, a level place was cleared out on the ground and the stones positioned in a circle about two steps wide. They then placed one stone in the middle of the ring. Jadan drew his sword and balanced its slender blade on the center rock. Released from his grip, the sword began slowly rotating until stopping then pointing toward the heart of Gravenwood.

"Following the sword would be our shortest path to Sentinel," Jerol remarked.

"You're right, Brother. Taking any other line would add days maybe even weeks to our journey. Besides, the forest is so enormous that our chances of running into the mound would be small. And to tell you the truth, I'm not sure I believe those stories about the mound anyway," Jadan replied.

"I know what you mean. Those tales about the mounds

were so fantastic. Surely they are fables," Jerol agreed.

(I had warned the boys many times about an ancient altar mound rising up from deep in Gravenwood's heart. Many similar mounds were scattered throughout Terrenea. Those who followed the Way of Light knew to avoid them. But, my sons did not always take me seriously).

So, the boys decided to follow the sword and plotted a course east-southeast and moved ahead.

"I hope Mother and Father are worried about us," Jadan said as the two marched deeper into the woods. "I sure was glad to get away from those two. I was beginning to feel as if I couldn't even breathe without Father giving me some kind of serious lecture, or Mother telling me to be careful or you'll get hurt!"

"Yes, Brother. Father can be a little longwinded sometimes," Jerol responded.

It was midday and everywhere they looked they could see huge columns of light shining through occasional openings in the covering above.

"Remember how mad Father got when he found out I had gone swinging on those vines over Sawtooth ravine? I thought he was going to really let me have it!" Jadan laughed.

"Yeah, I thought he was going to skin you alive. When he warns us not to do something and then we do it—That's when the hammer falls," Jerol quipped.

"Well, I'm glad I don't have to listen to his yakkin' anymore," Jadan remarked.

Jerol stopped. "Jadan, don't talk that way about Father. He may be longwinded, but his lectures have saved our hides more than once. I think we would be smart to consider that the Logos commands us to "Honor your father and your mother, so that your days in Terrenea may be long which Deus your King gives you" (Logos 2: 20:12).

"Yeah, yeah, whatever." Jadan waved with his hand.

Just then the boys were halted by two rain foxes and a braccon scurrying past in a frenzy. This was the boys' first encounter with these types of wildlife. Braccons are weasel-like creatures with solid black heads; rain foxes are known for their haunting cries during rain showers. Braccons are the favorite food of rain foxes. This was an unusual sight to see them so far back in the forest. Typically these species were only found on the prairies of Callow. And even more curious, the braccon was chasing the fox! Jerol and Jadan watched as the furry critters darted past them and out of sight. Before the brothers could say much, a couple of silver deer bounded past. Not far behind came a flock of prairie birds flying fast and through, dodging the low-lying limbs. The boys' attention was drawn back to the forest floor as three squawking tree hogs scampered by. Tree hogs—small rodents with sharp claws, resembling hairless guinea pigs—are tree dwellers and are unique to Gravenwood. Even the insects appeared to be moving to the center of the woods. Jerol knelt down to discover ants and bugs marching in one accord. Jadan ran ahead to see if he could spot anything out of the ordinary.

"See anything, Brother?" Jerol shouted.

"Nope, just a bunch of wild animals running from everywhere and all going in the same direction," Jadan reported.

Sin, who was rooting close by, stopped and lifted his head up, tilting it back and forth and listening to something the brothers' could not hear. The nervous pig became increasingly agitated and started squealing and grunting.

"Hey, what's the matter with your pig?" Jerol asked.

Jadan watched in bewilderment as Sin bolted off, disappearing into the forest. The woodland was abuzz with the noise of crawling, flying, running animals.

Jadan pointed at the woods. "Look, Jerol. Every creature in sight is going in the same direction." The brothers regrouped and scratched their heads.

"What do you think it means?" Jadan asked.

"I don't know, Brother. But I think it would a mistake to go in the same direction. Let me use the sword to help with our bearing. Perhaps we should chart another course to Sentinel." Jadan reluctantly agreed, even though still concerned about why Sin had left.

Jerol drew his sword and placed it on the center rock. At the beginning of their trip the sword had stopped, pointing in the direction of Sentinel. But this time the blade was spinning! When released from his grip, the blade began rotating slowly in a circle! This had never happened before. Utterly baffled, Jadan removed Jerol's sword and replaced it with his own. Just like his brother's, Jadan's blade began to spin.

"This doesn't make sense," Jerol remarked. "There is evidently some kind of strange force all around us. I suggest we change course and move to our right until we move beyond the curse on this place."

"Yeah. Well, I don't much care about makin' it to Sentinel right now," Jadan stated. "I've got to get to Sin before something bad happens to him." Jadan began walking away and in the direction of where he had last seen Sin.

"Jadan, wait! Not so fast! This is too strange to just take off without thinking it through. Who knows what's going on in there? Jerol pointed to the heart of the forest.

"Sorry, Brother. No time to talk. I'll catch up with you at Tryst Rock at the base of the Black Mountains. Give me six days. If I'm not at Tryst by then, come and get me." Jadan shouted as he disappeared into the distant shade.

Jerol felt a profound responsibility for his brother's welfare, but for them to walk into potential trouble would not be smart. "Jadan is clever. He knows what he's doing," Jerol thought. "He can take care of himself." So, Jerol decided to take a different line to the rendezvous point and wait. He felt that taking a different course than the animals would be his best bet of avoiding danger. And even though changing his track potentially meant a longer journey to the mountains, it was a sacrifice well worth making.

For the rest of that day Jadan followed the animals deeper into the woods. Night fell, but Jadan pushed on. With no moon to light his way, Jadan used his tortoise shell lamp. Even by lamplight the forest was spooky. He could hear the sounds of animals rustling across the ground and through the brush just beyond his circle of light. At one point the tired boy walked along the bank of a big pond and made a disturbing discovery. He found a heaping mound of fish, flipping and flopping, bunched up onto one bank of the pond. He watched in wonder as other fish continued jumping out of the water and onto the pile. Something was beckoning the animals. But what could it be? He walked on for a few more steps before giving in to his weary body. So he found a large hollowed out log, cleared out a good spot, and settled down for the night.

For the next two days, Jadan followed the parade deeper into Gravenwood. Around midafternoon on the second day, he looked up and thought he could see animals congregating in the distance. As he moved closer, he witnessed a sight that was beyond explanation. In the heart of the woodland the ground began to swell into an immense mound from which towered five enormous monoliths. Each rose skyward to the height of about two hundred hands and was about five steps wide at their base. From what Jadan could tell, they were made of solid white granite.

"This must be the altar mound. I remember what Father said about this place, but I've got to see with my own eyes if it is true," Jadan thought. Instead of running away, Jadan's curiosity took hold, pulling him closer to the mound. As he got closer he could see that four of the giant stones were graven in the shapes of animals. There was a lion, an eagle, a dragon and a tigerfish. All four were evenly spread out around a center monument.

The lion stood erect on its hind legs with front legs spread apart and paws open exposing claws. Its head was thrown back roaring to the sky. The eagle stood proudly, with head held high and wings folded back as though guarding its nest. The dragon rested on its hindquarters but with head falling down and mouth open wide. And lastly, the tigerfish was chasing its prey with mouth open wide yielding rows of jagged teeth.

The fifth statue, however, rose up in the center and was fashioned in the image of a Terrenean! The figure was broader at the base and stood taller than the others.

The monolith towered to a staggering height of about three hundred hands and was nearly twenty-five steps wide at its foundation! The impressive statue appeared to be in the likeness of a statesman dressed in ceremonial robe and champion's crown.

Standing about one hundred steps from the mound, Jadan could see the lion facing him. To the lion's left stood the dragon facing away from the center; to the lion's right was the eagle which also faced away from the center of the mound. The Terrenean statue stood in the center of the mound with its back to Jadan. Barely visible, beyond the center monolith, stood the tigerfish facing away from Jadan. Jadan looked with wonder at the scene before him. The air was filled with the noise of grunts, chirps, clicks, growls, and hissing as creatures of the forest continued their steady pilgrimage toward the mound. Fowl were flying in from every direction. Upon closer investigation, Jadan perceived that they were flocking to the eagle monolith.

The white eagle's head was grotesque, covered in bird droppings and countless motionless birds. Birds stood immobile covering every ledge of the statue with other birds hovering and searching for a place to land. Astonished, Jadan witnessed a couple of birds land and then stop as though frozen in ice! On the ground and encircling the statue's base lay a mat of countless bones and on top of the bones fluttered many additional fowl fighting for a place to sit. Jadan looked to his left to witness a similar scene at the dragon's stone. Snakes, turtles, and lizards were moving toward the dragon until they got to within about ten paces from the stone. Similar to the eagle, serpent bones lay scattered about the dragon's base covered by a myriad of motionless cold-blooded creatures. Jadan could see many scorpions and vipers coiled atop and hanging like hair from the top of the dragon's head.

Jadan looked back down to ground level and watched as nearly two hundred pigs moved near and around the statues. They were scattered across the mound, scurrying about eating, rutting, squealing, and grunting.

As he looked beyond the center stone, what he saw sent chills up his spine. Spread over a large area and posing like statues were the bodies and skeletons of people. The silent crowd stood locked in countless positions, many with shocked expressions and hands over their mouths. Even though there were as many unusual poses as there were people, there was still one eerie thing they had in common: Every single one of them appeared to be gazing up in the same direction. "What are they looking at?" Jadan questioned. They each appeared to be staring at the monolith in the center of the mound. "But why the statue of the Terrenean?" Jadan wondered.

Just then he spotted Sin among dozens of other busy swine plowing through some bones near the base of the lion. "Sin, Sin, over here!" Jadan shouted as he ran to his buddy. But Sin disregarded him and continued to dig. Jadan worked his way over, pushing and shoving animals out of his way. They seemed oblivious of his presence. "Sin, it's me. What's wrong with you?" Jadan heaved on Sin's back with all his might, but the stubborn pig merely ignored him and refused to budge. Jadan was concerned for Sin, but he knew that he needed to see if he could help the Terreneans. So, he hurried back to get a closer look.

Up close Jadan discovered that some people appeared to be starving and looked ill. Many looked as though they were close to death! "It's worse that I thought. I've got to do something and fast!" Jadan thought. He was in a most desperate situation. Jadan ran over to a young boy, not much older than himself, who was staring at the monolith with a sad look on his face. Jadan approached and, with his back to the statue, stood face to face with the listless child. Staring into the boy's glassy eyes for a sign of life, he tried to communicate. "Hello! Can you hear me?" A tear slowly formed, and then rolled from the corner of the boy's eye and down his ashen cheek. "Don't worry. I'll get you out of this!" Jadan tried to offer hope.

Jadan noticed that the boy's eyes did not move but stared straight ahead as though Jadan were not even there! As he circled around and behind the boy, the monument's face came into view. Instinctively Jadan looked up and into the eyes of the great statue. Like a god made of stone, the monolith was stately and regal with eyes of darkness. Instantly, he felt something like icicles forming inside his heart! His blood began to feel like ice water. With each heartbeat he could feel his body going to sleep! A deep alarming chill began spreading throughout his arms and legs. Frantic, he tried to look away, but could not. His body quickly grew cold and refused to move. Try as he might to pull away, it was too late. The mysterious monolith had claimed another captive. Jadan was in deep trouble.

Jerol had covered much territory since parting ways with Jadan. He had decided to move south, directly crossing the line of travel of the animals. He reasoned this would take him past the influence of the invisible force in the least amount of time. His decision was proved right when, in short order, he crossed through an area of the forest where animals were scurrying about in normal fashion. As he marched on, Jerol kept his mind off his brother by mentally measuring the shadows of the forest. Step by step he made his way toward Tryst. Soon, nightfall came. By the light of his lamp he found a large wigerroot tree. The wigerroot was known for its intricate root systems that fanned out from its base, weaving, forking, and twisting in and out of the ground creating many places where weary travelers could rest for the night. Tired but pleased, Jerol made camp for the evening. He found the perfect spot, cleaned out a space, and bedded down for a welcomed rest.

Jerol was awakened the next morning by cool water dripping onto his face. He opened and focused his eyes on a root a couple of hands above his face. There was a gentle morning rain soaking the trees' high canopy, creating small streams of water running down their ruddy trunks. Jerol listened as the drizzle gently brushed the trees, creating a sound like applause from a crowd. Jerol was cozy in his warm cloak. He did not want to get up and face the discomfort of being wet, but he knew he had better get going if he were going to get to Tryst on time. The rain continued off and on for the remainder of that day and night.

For five more days Jerol traveled before reaching the foothills of the Black Mountain. In the foothills, the trees were spaced farther apart, and the ground was clear of brush and vines. Jerol took about one more half day to reach the rendezvous point. But he had taken longer than he had expected to find the meeting place. Jerol looked around the rock, but found no sign of Jadan. He shouted for his brother, but with no response.

"It's been about six days since I last saw him," Jerol

thought. "He said he would meet me here in six days. Well, where is he? Hmm, he *is* late most of the time, so I think I had better wait a little longer before I get too worried."

Jerol did not want to overreact. He decided to set up camp. He decided that he would wait a couple more days for his brother and Sin to show up. But after waiting for only one day, Jerol could delay no longer.

"He should be here by now. I chose a path that circled around the woodland's heart while Jadan moved straight through. I think he could have made it in four days." Jerol wondered.

Fueled by growing concern for his brother's welfare, Jerol hurriedly broke camp, pulled up his gear, and plunged back into the woods.

He had only been traveling for about a day when he came back across the march of the spellbound animals. He had decided to follow them in hopes they would lead him to Jadan. As he made his trek deeper into the forest, Jerol began to spot many trees that were dead or dying. More and more patches of barren areas began to appear, where the trees had died and lost their foliage, scarring the heart of the woodland. Eventually there was no underbrush, just dying trees and ground that was cracked from an occasional rain and constant heat from the sun. The once beautiful landscape was becoming almost inhospitable.

The anxious boy continued to follow the creatures until he saw, between the many lines of lifeless tree trunks, what looked to be a mound of some sort with an outcropping of colossal stone about three hundred steps away. Jerol stopped; something did not look right. He had not seen much rock on the forest floor during his journey from Tryst. Now he was looking at tons of rock jutting high out of the ground in one spot. "Oh no, it looks like Father knew what he was talking about. I've found the altar mound," Jerol thought. Cautiously, he retrieved his spyglass to get a closer look before moving ahead. As he focused the instrument, the first image was a group of people and skeletons standing with their backs to him!

Jerol felt a lump grow in his throat. He quickly moved his view to the standing stone nearest to him. He was surprised to see a massive carving of a dragon covered with writhing snakes. He looked down at its massive base at piles of bones covered in a mass of many serpents. He quickly shifted his attention in the direction of the center monolith where he spotted Jadan standing behind another boy! Jadan appeared to be looking up and intently at something.

Curious, Jerol moved his glass to investigate further. He looked past Jadan to the base of the monument. The image was blurry so Jerol twisted his glass into focus. He then began moving his view up its side. What he saw was a colossal statue of some dignitary sculpted from beautiful white granite! A remarkable sight to see—a monument of such gigantic proportions carved from a material as hard as white stone. The detail of the art was magnificent. He could see that the figure was dressed in royal clothes and jewels and held something that looked like a scepter in one hand. He continued panning up the statue's long figure to see its face. First he saw a mouth, then the nose, and then…

Unexpectedly, his view was blocked by something that had moved into his line of sight. Startled, he jerked his eye away from the end of the glass to find Prayer standing about halfway between him and the towering monolith. The graceful bird stood tall with wings spread wide apart. "What is he doing?" Jerol wondered. "It looks like he's trying to shield me from something." Sensing danger, Jerol began to quickly piece together what he had just seen. The gigantic sculptures of stone appeared to be idols, and the crowd of lifeless people were looking at them. Instantly, Jerol flashed back in his memory to the full story his grandfather had told him back in Agog about the land of ancient times. Jerol had thought the tale to be a legend, but by the looks of things, it just might be true.

Ages ago, after the Terreneans had been cast out of Shalom, for protection many began assembling into large groups. Usually a group would form around someone or something that had performed an act of heroism. For example, a few gathered in the name of the eagle, for some people said that they had witnessed eagles bringing fish to their starving village during a season of drought. Another group gathered to honor the lion, for lions had been seen saving children from stalking bears.

But in reality, Azrael had staged these elaborate rescues in the hopes that Terrenea would turn their trust to false leaders and away from the King. Azrael had directed his minions to wear an animal disguise and carry out the deceitful deeds. Steadily, the Evil Lord's plan began to take hold, and before long those who were gullible erected massive graven images to honor their new protectors and providers.

Summer after summer, people in increasing numbers began to turn away from King Deus and rely on their creature gods, until one day a Terrenean named Eidolon* rose up among the people, doing many greats deeds of valor. His fame spread as he helped the sick, encouraged the downcast, and stood up for the homeless and hurting. Azrael watched with interest as Eidolon's influence with Terrenea began to grow.

When the time was right, the evil Shadow King offered Eidolon a deal. "If you will serve me, then I will give you anything your heart desires." A covenant was made, and Azrael set in motion what he hoped would seal his victory over the King. The conniving con orchestrated a plan where Eidolon would team up with the beloved creature gods to rule over Mankind. Once the people had pledged their allegiance to Eidolon, Eidolon would point to Azrael, his true source of power. Azrael then would appear and seize the Kingdom. Before long, just as Azrael had foreseen, the Terreneans erected a monolith to worship Eidolon that towered above all others! Nature no longer held their highest praise. The image they worshipped was that of their own kind. At last, Azrael had gotten what he had wanted. He had diverted most of Terrenea's attention away from the King and onto itself. Across the land, monoliths were erected one by one until most of Terrenea worshipped a graven god. Almost everything in Terrenea was turned into graven icons of every shape and form.

At last, with most Terreneans playing along, Azrael could take his plan to its final stage. He would infuse the eyes of the monoliths with idolatry, the purest form of iniquity. Its evil essence was so cold that it could freeze Terreneans in their tracks, rendering them useless to the King! Even though most of my race followed Eidolon, there was still a small group who refused to acknowledge him as king. They stood fast in the hope that their place in the Kingdom would one day be restored and their way of life would return just as in the days of Shalom. These warriors of light took seriously the King's warning: "You shall not make to yourselves any graven image, or any likeness of anything that is in the heavens above, or that is in Terrenea beneath, or that is in the water under the ground. You shall not bow yourself down to them, nor serve them. For I Deus your King am a jealous King"(Logos 2:20:4,5). Because of the courage of these few, to this day Azrael has not been able to fully claim Deus' kingdom for his own. According to the fable, ancient shrines are still scattered throughout Terrenea, working to capture those who have lost faith in the King.

Jerol was convinced that he had found the ancient shrine of Eidolon in the heart of Gravenwood. The mound was no myth! If he dared to look at Eidolon's eyes, idolatry would claim his soul and he would become useless as the living dead. Without the ability to move, he would starve and die. Over time, all that would be left would be his bones.

Jerol was not sure how long Jadan had been trapped without food or water. He knew he must find a way to break the curse, for time was of critical importance. Jerol wanted to run in and rescue his brother, but he knew if he tried in his own strength he would be overcome by the curse of the mound. So, he made sure to avoid eye contact with the monolith and with his mind racing, turned his back to the mound, sat down, and closed his eyes, searching his heart for a plan. The answer came quickly. Prayer is immune to idolatry! The awesome bird is a Royal falcon! Azrael's evil magic could not taint his regal blood.

Jerol immediately stood up and waved at his friend who remained faithfully shielding him from danger. Even though Jerol stood many steps away from Prayer, the mighty falcon could see him with perfect clarity. Jerol began communicating with his friend by using hand and arm signals. The royal warrior was trained well and knew exactly what to do. Confident that Prayer would deliver, Jerol sat back down and turned facing away from the mound. With a burst of power, the falcon shot up and into the sky, circled out and back, then flew down, landing on top of the statue's head. He then spread out his wide graceful wings and pushed them down, covering Eidolon's face from view. Prayer screamed out a high shrill, telling Jerol that he could approach the mound.

Jerol knew that he did not have much time and moved in a beeline to his brother. Released from the curse's control, Jadan slowly began to slump. The boy in front of Jadan fell to the ground. Jadan's arms fell to his sides, and then he collapsed as well. People around them began falling in heaps upon the ground! The sacred mound began filling with the noise of swine and animals combined with the voices of moaning people. Jerol knelt down next to his brother and cradled him in his arms. Jadan had lost much weight. Jerol hurriedly pulled his water bag from his pack and placed its spout on his brother's parched lips. At first he refused to drink, but in no time he was gulping so hard that Jerol had to pull the bag away.

Once Jerol was satisfied that he had properly tended to his brother, he began running to and sharing his water with as many others as he could. Some were sick. But, for some, help had come too late, for many were dead. Overwhelmed, Jerol made rounds caring for as many as he could find. He ran to his pack, pulled out and began rationing every bit of his food and honey among the afflicted. While Jerol was rushing from person to person, Prayer screeched again. Jerol looked up. "What is it, boy?" The vigilant bird turned his head to the west. Jerol looked to see eleven boys walking through the mound area, looking around with puzzled expressions etched on their faces.

Jerol immediately stood and began waving in big motions, running to warn them. "Stay back! Stay back! Stay away from the mound!" Jerol shouted. The startled boys stopped and drew their swords. "My name is Jerol. My brother and I were on our way to Sentinel when he was cursed by the enchanted stone. Many more were already here when I arrived. As you can see, my falcon has broken the spell and I am trying to help as many as I can."

One of the boys sheathed his blade and stepped forward. "I am Sanguine* and also heading for Sentinel." The other boys dropped their guard and made hasty introductions as well. "How can we help?" they asked.

"Those of you who have food and drink, go to the hurting. Get as much nourishment in them as they'll take," Jerol responded. "Many are weak. Some are ill. We must move them to safety as quickly as we can, for night will soon be upon us and my falcon can only stand guard for so long."

"Perhaps our falcons can help as well," Sanguine offered as he lifted up a beautiful ruby hanging from his neck. He moved the crimson gem through the sunlight and signaled overhead. Four of the others signaled as well, two with whistles and one by clicking two clear stones together. Almost immediately five great birds flying in level and at a fast rate of speed appeared from just above the tree tops, diving down to join the group. Shul*, Psalter*, Rue*, Pantheon* and Chantry* were Royal falcons! None were as large as Prayer, but each was well trained and ready to fight. Sanguine and the others gave the signals, and the magnificent fowl took their positions, blocking the monoliths from view. Frightened by the feathered fighters, Sin and the other hogs scattered in every direction, squealing into the woods.

The boys broke up and began helping the hurting. Jadan was weak but recovered more quickly than most. Once he had regained his strength, he began ministering aid to the boy who had collapsed beside him. The boy was thin and close to death. Jadan carried him to safety and began to give him water. "Thank…you…" the boy whispered.

"Save your strength and take this food." Jadan encouraged.

"What…is…your name?" the boy whispered.

"Jadan. What's yours?"

"Xeno*." The weary boy replied, and then collapsed. Those who were able were carried out one by one to a designated area just out of sight of the altar mound. Many trips were made as the boys worked well into the night, by torchlight, until everyone was brought to safety.

Jerol directed the other boys: "Sanguine, have some of your friends build campfires for the night. Position ten of the injured around each fire. The rest of you come with me to gather food and water."

"Thank you for saving our lives," Sanguine replied. "Without your warning, I fear what might have happened to us. King Deus would be proud, for you represent him well."

"No, I owe you thanks. For without your help, many would be lost. Because of you and your good falcons, over a hundred will live to be with their families again," Jerol responded.

Sanguine and two others built twelve fires straight away and moved the injured around them just as Jerol had instructed. Jerol and the rest returned at daybreak with enough food and water to last a couple more days. Each day the ailing grew stronger until they in turn cared for those around them. Because everyone pitched in, the sick were able to regain enough strength to leave the camp in about five days. Of the one hundred and nine that were rescued from the mound, only seven did not survive.

One by one and sometimes in pairs, the thankful strangers left the safety of the campsite. Sanguine and Shul in time moved on, as did his friends and their falcons. They each promised to find Jadan and Jerol once they arrived in Sentinel. Xeno fully recovered in a couple of days and stayed helping others until he was the last to leave. He vowed that someday he would repay his obligation to Jadan, Jerol, and the others.

Finally, it was back to Jadan and Jerol. The grateful brothers wasted no time in setting their course out of Gravenwood. Retracing his steps, Jerol led them back out of the forest and along the Black Foothills to Tryst Rock.

"Well, Jadan. We made it," Jerol offered with a look of relief. Jadan seemed preoccupied in thought, staring at the mountains, and did not say anything. Once at Tryst they climbed to its flat top and sat looking up at the colossal mountain range between them and Malevolence. The Black Mountains looked down on the tiny brothers as though daring them to pass.

"Looks like a long road ahead, Brother," Jadan replied. Jerol nodded his head in agreement and looked at his brother with thankfulness for a second opportunity. The grateful brothers were humbled by their ordeal in Gravenwood and understood that without Prayer they would have been doomed. Jerol's ever-watchful friend had given them the ability they needed to turn their backs on the shrine and its curse. The brothers had learned their lessons; they would avoid idolatry at all costs. No matter what lay ahead, they would turn their attention back to the Crossing and march on.

Chapter 7

Malevolence

"Travel on the narrow path. For wide and broad is the road that leads to trouble, and many travel on it, but small is the trail and narrow the path that leads to Sentinel, and only a few find it." Logos 40:7:13

The Black Mountains stood in somber silence before the determined brothers. Jadan had advanced several steps ahead of Jerol. They stood visually surveying the rocky landscape. Jadan spotted a strange opening in the mountain's side and promptly reported his discovery back to Jerol. "Look, Jerol. Over there! It looks like a way through!" Jadan shouted pointing to the North.

As they moved closer to the mountain's toe, they were halted by yawning ravines that had been carved into the softer ground by runoff flowing swiftly from the steep sides of the mountain. Luckily the gullies were dry, and the brothers were able to climb down, through, and then up the other side until standing at the rock-strewn toe of the mountain. There they quickly found the opening that Jadan had spotted earlier. The passageway was running between two monstrous sections of stone. It looked as if a gigantic axe had fallen on the mountain's rim creating a plunging gash from top to bottom. The brothers cautiously followed the odd corridor through the mountain until exiting on the opposite side before a vast open plain.

The brothers looked at each other with expressions of surprise. What they feared would be a great test of their endurance had turned out to be an easy hike. "Guess that goes to show you, brother. Don't worry until you have a reason to worry," Jerol observed.

"Yeah, sometimes what looks like a mountain turns out to be the easiest way to travel," Jadan replied. They each checked their maps and concluded that they had found Malevolence* (*Plain of Gall**).

Malevolence was reputed to be a lonely place, a sprawling valley surrounded by the uneven Black Mountains on two sides, the Mirth Mountains to the North, and the Backbiter Mountains on the east side. The territory was mostly flat, with great open fields of waist high yellow grass, sprinkled with a few groves of wild pepper berry bushes.

Before long the trail split into two dissimilar pathways. One was wide and clear, worn and showing evidence of countless travelers. The other path, however, was narrow, rough, and wild with tangled vines.

The brothers stopped and stood in silence studying their choices. "Well, the best way to me is obvious. Come on, follow me," Jadan barked as he hoisted his gear, winked, and quickly headed down the wide road with Sin hurrying to catch up. "Anybody with half a mind can see that the way traveled by the most people has got to be the best way to go!"

"Not so quick!" Jerol retorted. "Remember what the Scrolls teach about the broad road? 'Broad is the road that leads to trouble'" (Logos 40:7:13).

Jadan stopped and looked back in disbelief. "Jerol, my dear brother, it is clear to me that you've been spending way too much time listening to fairy tales! Open your eyes!" He pointed down the disheveled footpath. "You can't even see down that way! It will take you the rest of today just to go twenty steps! Sometimes you've got to use a little common sense and not be so naïve."

Jerol was not impressed by his brother's lecture. "Yes, Jadan, I know it looks impossible, but I'll choose to take the King's advice instead of yours any day. If you keep going down the way you have chosen, then you better beware. I think it looks too good to be true. Be careful, Brother!"

Jadan smirked, laughing. "Hey, suit yourself. Sin and I will be waiting for you in Sentinel. Well, that is, if you ever make it there!" With that, Jadan motioned good-bye and hurried down the broad road and out of sight.

Disagreements like this between Jerol and Jadan were nothing new. They rarely agreed on anything lately. Leaving Jadan to his devices, Jerol focused his attention back to the narrow way. He studied the twisted curtain of vines hanging before him. "Well, I've got plenty of work to do," he thought. "The earlier I start, the sooner I'll finish."

Jerol drew his sword and began hacking at the stubborn mat of thin cords. They hung so thickly that he was only able to go a few steps at a time. Little by little, Jerol cut his way through the tangled mess, as Prayer faithfully flew watch overhead. Jerol was determined, no matter how hard the struggle might be, he would do whatever the King commanded.

Chapter 8

Brawlers

"You child of Azrael, you enemy of all that is good. Won't you stop twisting the good ways of the King?"
Logos 44:13:10

Jadan and Sin had crossed much ground since parting ways with Jerol and were feeling proud of themselves. Traveling on the wide road was smooth. "If the rest of the trip is as easy as this, I'll get to Sentinel in no time!" he proudly thought. However, little did he know that his day was about to take a huge turn for the worse.

It was midmorning when Jadan decided that he and Sin would stop and take a short break. He settled down atop a soft mossy stump on the bank of a clear brook and took a cool drink of water. Sin began rooting under the stump for some tasty swamp worms. But, Jadan had a dangerous habit of dropping his guard. As he savored the refreshing mountain water, out of the surrounding brush leaped a Brawler*!

Pear-shaped with a small chest, the Brawler had a

knobby head and a rounded, spongelike belly that spilled over his belt on every side. His long, thick hairy arms dragged the ground as he lumbered to and fro. A wide, frizzy, red beard covered most of his wrinkled face and hid his belly when he stood at rest.

Brawlers were angry creatures. They were mostly loners—wandering souls, bullies who were irritated at life, mean, and vicious. Because of their unusual appearance, unkind Terreneans would often tease them. They had developed unhealthy ways of coping by carrying clubs and spears. They were known for the use of various poisons. Whenever they used clubs, they would soak them for days in a vat filled with black henbane, the poison of hate.

The menacing intruder stood at a distance, glaring at Jadan. Still kneeling by the brook, Jadan spotted a tall slender spear, tightly clasped in the Brawler's left hand. Sin was no help; he ran off through the bushes squealing like, well, a pig!

The Brawler scowled and grumbled something under his breath, and then began hobbling toward the startled boy! Fearing his threatening manner, Jadan gradually stood up searching his surroundings, considering an escape. Even though the boy stood slightly taller, the Brawler was thicker and wider!

But when the Brawler got to within a few steps of Jadan, he stopped again and stood studying Jadan's unsheathed sword. Slowly, Jadan backed away, hoping to avoid confrontation. But in a flash, the Brawler thrust his spear! The tip of the spear had been dipped in scalding sarcasm, a blistering agent used often by the Brawlers. Jadan tried to dodge the point, but he was knocked backward and onto the ground as the spear struck him squarely on his unprotected right shoulder.

Jadan reached up, wrestling the spear from the Brawler's cluthes and quickly threw the dull stick into the bushes! Surprised by the boy's quick reflexes, the Brawler stumbled away just long enough for Jadan to crouch down onto one knee behind his shield.

Fortunately for Jadan, the spear had not been designed to kill. The poison on its dull end, however, caused aggravating irritation. Almost immediately, Jadan began to sense a wave of anxiety moving throughout his body.

The Brawler came back again, this time swiping low with a dagger, trying to get at the boy's left heel, which was exposed just below the bottom of the shield. The Brawler's aim was precise and the dagger found its mark. The pain was immediate, jolting Jadan back onto the ground! The knife's dull edge had been laced with ergot, another potent poison of violence.

As usual Sin stayed hidden in the shadows, trying hard to remain silent and unnoticed. The Brawler pressed in closer toward Jadan who was hopping and scrambling to regain his balance. Jadan felt fury rush up and overtake him. He jumped up and made a dash to retrieve his weapon from beside the stump. He scooped the sword up and began flailing it wildly as he ran at the laughing Brawler.

Jadan's explosive reaction, however, was exactly what the cunning Brawler had hoped for. The desperate boy's out-of-control display of rage and fear was a sure sign that the Brawler's poison was working. If Jadan had only remembered that sarcasm and ergot are often used to induce intense anger, which produces an error of judgment, then perhaps his response would have been more measured.

The Brawler's poisons were weak, and, believe it or not, could be overcome by ignoring the feelings they induced. You see, had Jadan remained calm and ignored the Brawler's threats, his attacker would have sooner or later lost interest and halted his advance.

Brawlers do not measure their success by the physical wounds they cause, but instead by the fear and anger they perceive in their victims. Rarely does a Brawler try to kill his victim. Instead, he displays physical aggression and injects evil poisons in hopes of causing anger and fear. The more anger or fear he senses, the meaner and bolder he becomes. However, more often than not, if his victim shows little regard for his challenge, he will sulk and walk away. Thus, the best defense against a Brawler is to turn and walk away from him. This tactic immediately deflates the Brawler's sense of control. However, I must warn you, there are times when a Brawler's attack is so fierce that meeting him with equal or greater force is needed. The aim is to remain in control and not push back out of fear or anger, but from self-preservation.

Jadan had been drawn into battle for the wrong reasons. When the dust had settled, the bulb-shaped bully was nowhere to be found and Jadan lay blistered and battered on the road.

After peering out in every direction, Sin wobbled out from the brush and next to Jadan's side. He was glancing from side to side, and nervously began prodding Jadan in the back with his wet, cold snout as if to say, "Why are you just lying there? Get up! Let's get out of here!"

Jadan, in no mood for Sin's lack of concern, lifted his head from the ground and blasted the jittery swine with angry words. "You big fat slob! Where were you while I was being beaten up? If I could, I'd get up *and* toss you in the creek! Maybe that would wake you up to the fact there are others in this world besides your old grimy, good-for-nothin' self!"

Sin pranced back through the bushes squealing with nose and tail pointed skyward. He was obviously unappreciative of Jadan's truthful remarks!

In consequence of Jadan's tussle with the Brawler, Jadan was worn out and had lost valuable time. Perhaps if he had not reacted so predictably, the damage could have been avoided. Regrettably, his recuperation would take days.

Elsewhere, the satisfied Brawler proudly reported back to Mount Sheol*. "Master, the plan worked just as you predicted! The silly boy has been detained." Not saying a word, Azrael gave a crooked smirk, turned, and silently slithered back into the shadows.

Chapter 9

The Badger Winds

"Be on the lookout. Stand firm in the faith. Be a man. Be strong." Logos 47:16:13

Jerol was getting accustomed to hacking his way through endless rows of thorn-infested underbrush. The work was hard and even discouraging at times, but Jerol never flinched. He kept on going. In some places the narrow path was totally blocked, taking days to advance only a few steps!

One particular morning had started out well. Jerol finished consulting the Scrolls for clues of where the keys might be found. The sun was projecting light beams through the clouds and onto the early morning mist. Birds were singing cheerful melodies weaving a tapestry of beautiful music. As Jerol sat marveling at the splendor of the new day, he noticed a group of black clouds that was moving in over the northern ridge of the Mirth Mountains.

The clouds rapidly blanketed the sky, obscuring most of the daylight. Before long the sky grew dark, and a chilly wind began to stir. Jerol heard a rushing sound above him and looked up. A group of black-bellied clouds were spinning directly above. They were each lit up on the inside like giant sacks filled with fireflies. The flashes of soft pale light painted the plain in muted colors of yellow and orange. Jerol was unable to see the dangerous whirlwinds of popular culture hiding deep inside the boiling billows. Like a swarm of angry hornets, they could quickly move out, changing the landscape in the blink of an eye.

Azrael had learned ages ago how to seed the clouds with deception whenever he wanted to cause widespread damage to the land below.

Jerol could feel a lukewarm breeze start to push against him. It was weak at first, but steadily grew into a powerful gust filling the air with dust and leaves. He watched as two trees next to him began to gradually bend under the load. Jerol crouched low to the ground and held onto a sturdy pepperberry bush. "Hey, don't go that way! Come on, follow us! We know a better way! Come on!" Jerol searched the shadows of the plain to see who was talking, but no one was there. "Over here! What are you waiting for?" The voices called out above the noise of the wind.

Turning in circles and searching in all directions, Jerol shouted, "Who are you?"

"Don't ask questions," came the reply. "Just follow us."

Yes, he was lonely, but Jerol was not willing to change his direction without a good reason. He knew he was on a quest, and he was determined to follow the way spelled out in the Scrolls. "No offense to whomever you are, but I already know where I want to go." Jerol could hear grumbling coming from somewhere back in the brush. He strained to see who was there, but all he could see were rustling bushes and vines.

"Who needs you anyway? Just like we thought, you are a strange fellow!" "You know, we never liked you anyway!" Another voice shouted out. "Hey, where'd ya get those elf ears?" "You're nothin' but skin and bones!" "Why don't you dress like us?" "What's wrong, little boy? What are you afraid of?" Apparently, Jerol had stumbled into a nest of Naysayers, a tight group of Terrenean bullies. During good weather, Naysayers were rarely seen. But when the storms blow in, that is their favorite time to come out of hiding and begin their dirty work. Their favorite activity is shunning those who do not agree with them and constantly harassing, badgering, and putting down those who do not join their group.

Jerol stuck his fingers in his ears and struggled to ignore their hurtful words. He was beginning to feel alone and he could hear voices whispering and laughing from everywhere. "Am I dreaming?" he wondered. He began to feel like an outcast, a misfit. He felt utterly alone and wanted only to go home.

In a flash a tremendous bolt of lightning cut down from the circling clouds! Jerol instinctively pulled his shield above his head and fell beneath its sturdy frame. The white-hot beam slammed dead center against its metal causing an ear splitting boom that violently shook the plain.

Jerol was driven down hard onto his back. Fortunately, the shield had deflected the lightning's destructive power. "What next?" he wondered.

At that moment the noise stopped, and the heavens opened up, releasing buckets of insults and slander*! From the looks of it, the storm was going to be a rough one.

As Jerol struggled to his feet, he was ankle deep in a layer of gravely ice. The ground began to tremble, and the firm soil on which he was standing began to shift and sway! His feet began sinking through a grey gooey mess! As the hailstones pummeled him from every direction, Jerol slung his shield to one shoulder and pulled his sword. Acting quickly, he then thrust its point with all his might into the shifting mess between his feet. Its metal slid easily through the hail and slimy muck, halting with a muffled "THUNK"!

His trusted blade sank up to its handle before stopping against something solid. In haste, and in a display of amazing skill, Jerol miraculously balanced his shield on top of the sword's handle, making a platform supported on solid rock above the ice and mud. Then he climbed on top of it, covering up with his heavy, waterlogged cloak. Incredibly, the shield locked tight onto the sword's sturdy handle. Jerol struggled to keep his balance, kneeling down and bowing his head, as the merciless barrage continued to hammer down.

Suddenly, the ground beneath him collapsed with a mighty rumble. Jerol dropped down and landed spread-eagle on the platform, grabbing tightly onto the sides of the shield. His saturated cloak was so heavy that it helped anchor him down. The platform vibrated and rocked so violently that Jerol's vision was blurred. He wanted to cover his ears but dared not release his grip.

When the squall had finally blown out and all was quiet again, Jerol cautiously peered out from underneath the dripping edge of his cloak. His eyes began to widen in disbelief as he stared up through a transparent sky of light blue. There were no clouds, no wind. The sun was blazing through the air brighter than he had ever seen before. He could see Prayer soaring and calling out from high above.

When Jerol looked down, however, his eyes grew even wider with surprise. Steam was beginning to rise from the soil as the hot sun met with the cold ice. The ground had caved in at least sixty hands beneath him on every side. He was left sitting high atop an uneven pinnacle of solid rock jutting stubbornly from a huge, ugly hole. The torrential downpour had eaten away a sizable section of land that once encircled the rock creating a gaping sinkhole that was at least one hundred steps across!

The aftermath of insults and slander always left an ugly scar on the land, and this was no exception. As far as Jerol could see, the Plain had been transformed into a sea of countless sinkholes. The storm's run-off cut a maze of small channels down the steep slopes of the bowl-shaped pit. They meandered across its bottom before disappearing through a dozen or so washed out holes at the base of the lofty rock upon which Jerol sat.

While Jerol scanned the landscape, flashes of light coming from the floor of the pit caught his attention. He strained to focus, but he was too far away to make out exactly what he was seeing. He climbed down the face of the rock and walked over to inspect. Only a fraction of the object was exposed to view. He knelt down to get a closer look then gently scooped away the mud, revealing some sort of odd stick. Bit by bit, he began to see what looked like gold! The object was roughly half a hand long with a handle the size of a baby's fist. As he stared with wonder and twirled it before his eyes, a rainbow of colors danced upon the object's smooth metallic surface.

"This must be an old spoon, lost by a Royal traveler many moons ago," Jerol reasoned to himself. He brought the item closer to his eyes. Etched into the face, and on each side of the handle, was the word "COURAGE." Jerol was stunned. He had found the key of courage! Conquering his doubt and using his sword to find solid ground, Jerol had survived the full force of the Badger* winds. Because of his bravery, he had been granted the key of courage!

Jerol could hardly believe his eyes. He had in his hands one of the four keys to Sentinel's door! He began leaping with joy, splashing mud and water everywhere! He danced and danced until he could dance no more! After placing his new key on a special ring on the sword's handle, Jerol called for Prayer to send a note to the King, telling him the exciting news!

The violent storm had taken its toll on the young lad, but he somehow found enough will to make his way back up the sinkhole's slippery side and out of the muddy pit. He was exhausted and decided to take a break for the remainder of the day.

Reclining on a soft layer of pepperberry leaves at the base of a large bush, Jerol began daydreaming about the next part of his quest. He recalled being told that another key might be found in a desert which lay on the outskirts of Malevolence, just on the other side of the Backbiter Mountains.

Jerol figured that if he started now, the trip would take at least a couple of seasons before he could get there. So, instead of forging ahead, he decided to rest and prepare his heart. "Today was a good day." He thought. Tomorrow he would walk.

Elsewhere, Jadan and Sin were still traveling on the wide road. Most days were filled with fighting and quarreling with more Brawlers. Word quickly spread throughout Malevolence that there was an easy target headed to Mammon. Within days, a group of Naysayers had tracked down Jadan and detained him for several weeks. Eventually, he escaped. But, before long he was confronted by a different brand of snobbish bullies known as the Judges.

The Judges are tall and scrawny Terreneans who wear small, round spectacles that sit balanced on the ends of their long, pointy noses. They arch their long backs and strut through Malevolence, staring down their "sniffers" at everyone they meet. On the surface they appear harmless, but without warning they can lash out with cruel whips of prejudice at anyone who crosses them. They swagger as they walk with puffed out chests, shaking their heads from side to side.

To Jadan the Judges were even more annoying than Brawlers and Naysayers combined. They were experts at entangling folks in arguments about the most insignificant nonsense. On several occasions, while traveling with Jadan, these rude blokes had the nerve to openly express their personal opinions about him. "Look at the way he's dressed. He's simply detestable. No self-respecting Terrenean would be caught dead in a wrap like that. I don't know why he can't be like us. How did his parents let him down? Look at how he carries himself. Quickly, let's move ahead of him before we are spotted together and mistaken as his friend."

In due course the Judges would move past. But to Jadan's dismay, another group of two or three would catch up from behind and another round of insults would begin. He tried to avoid them by stopping to rest. But every time, sooner or later another group would appear. To Jadan their criticisms were inescapable. But, instead of believing that he was just as important as other Terreneans, Jadan cared too much about what the Judges thought. He allowed their opinions to control him.

While on the Plain of Gall, Jadan stayed unhappy most of the time. His anger and insecurity had blinded him to the fact he and Sin had been walking in circles!

Periodically, Prayer would show up with a note of encouragement from Jerol. But the pig was jealous of Prayer's power and would always chase him away! Jadan repeatedly ignored the well wishes of his brother. He was just too absorbed in self-pity to respond.

It took awhile, but, thanks to the encouragement from several letters filled with brotherly concern, Jadan began to miss Jerol's company. Gradually, his stubborn will softened, and he decided to return to the trail in hopes of catching up with his brother. Ready to try again, Jadan set his sights on the Backbiter Mountains.

Chapter 10

The Keys

"I will give him complete authority under Me, he will have the keys to Sentinel. What he opens, no one will shut, and what he shuts no one will open." LOGOS 23:22:22

Azrael was so mean that he had made a special vow to stop every boy from becoming a Blade. To do this, he committed a sizable part of his forces to deceiving and entangling unsuspecting boys in webs of temptation, hoping to prevent them from finding the keys.

His reasoning was simple. If he could hinder enough boys from entering Sentinel, he would greatly enhance his odds of deposing the King and finally achieving his main goal—destroying the Kingdom of Light and claiming Mankind as slaves! So twisted was Azrael's heart that he had written the names of fatherless boys at the top of his target list. He knew that without the guidance of a loving father, a young boy could be helpless prey, distracted and easily tricked into wandering off course and away from Mettle's codes of honor. Sadly, the lives of many fatherless boys have been ruined by the demon's plan.

But to Azrael's dismay, there have been a few of the "fatherless" who have been able to unravel the Dark Lord's schemes, and despite overwhelming odds have succeeded in finding the keys and making their way onto the King's court. These inspiring young boys found their way by following their wiser peers or heeding sound advice of another boy's father. They hold a special place in Deus' heart because of their extraordinary courage and toughness.

In puzzling contrast there have been many other boys who, even though they had fathers, still chose to avoid Sentinel! Perhaps their fathers did not understand their sons' need for help and guidance. Perhaps their fathers had not seen the value of the Mark. Whatever the reason, scores of boys through the ages have missed out on the blessings of finding their utmost destiny.

Perhaps, before we go much farther, I should expand on the keys and their origin and meaning. Learning about the history of the keys will help you understand the daily battle that rages between Azrael and the Kingdom of Light.

As I have shared before, besides receiving Paladin's gift and the rite of Gehorsam, each boy must complete a third and final objective of the Crossing—collecting the four keys of Sentinel. This task requires more than just making a decision to look for them. It requires a new way of life. Rather than taking days to find them, locating the keys usually takes several summers of diligent searching.

The keys' purpose is to release four locks holding shut the enormous door of Sentinel. These locks were not part of the King's original plan, but are just another device of aggravation created by the Demon Lord.

As part of his plan of hate, Azrael would fasten four locks to Sentinel's only gate. However, before placing the locks on the city's door, he would test them on the gates of Sheol. He labored feverishly for endless days and nights blending and experimenting with different amounts of raw materials until discovering the right combination. The locks were crafted from a secret mix of black coal*, greenstone*, rusty iron*, and silver traprock*. He meticulously carved out each lock from the magical ore and welded them on Sheol's gate, using fire from his fingertips! For extra insurance, the eager Dragon dispatched four of his most trusted friends to stay near the gate and guard his locks. The spirit of Apathy perched tightly on top of the first lock in a vice-like grip. The demon of Fear sat patiently, waiting on top of another and had the apparatus fully wrapped with its boney tail. Qualm remained hidden between the lock and the gate where no one could see him while the sprite of Chicane clutched to the last one nervously waiting and watching.

Azrael thought to himself, "If these locks are sturdy enough to keep my mighty minions from getting out of Sheol, then I know that they will be tough enough to keep little boys from getting into Sentinel!" After many days of testing he was convinced, the locks would not fail. So, he rushed to Sentinel and personally installed the locks on the lofty door. Before returning to Sheol, he gave his slaves strict orders to guard the door with their lives.

The Dark Lord was convinced that he had a foolproof plan, but as usual the resourceful King had a better idea. When Deus learned of Azrael's scheme, in a surprising twist, he allowed the locks to remain on the door. As unlikely as it may seem, the King did not want each boy's passage to be trouble-free. Instead, our Lord planned to use the locks as a test of each boy's loyalty to him.

Knowing that the latches would be too strong for boys to break on their own, Deus created four special keys for each boy to use to unlock them. They were the keys of courage, integrity, service and vision. Each key was crafted from royal metals and plated with the purest gold. Each boy would have to find the set of keys made just for him, for the King had hidden them throughout Callow.

When Azrael learned that the Deus had created keys

for his locks, he became outraged and immediately summoned his army's chief demon.

"Sabaist*!" Azrael shouted.

"Yes, my master." The trembling slave bowed low in his usual position; facedown with arms fully extended.

"I have an important mission for you."

"Yes, your majesty. Your will is my desire."

"It has been brought to my attention that our cursed enemy has hidden keys somewhere in Terrenea. And apparently, he has placed them there to help his frail little friends release the locks I've placed upon Sentinel's gate!"

"Yes, my lord." The demon dared not look up.

Azrael, visibly agitated, turned his beady, glowing gaze toward Terrenea and quickly raised a pointing finger. "Go, Sabaist. Take as many legions of my best warriors as you need. Go quickly and don't come back until you have the keys. Do you understand?" Azrael slammed his clenched fist on the armrest of his throne and stood straight up, glaring down at his cowering crony. The war room shook violently. "Bring back every single key!"

"As you wish, my lord." The trembling demon slid backwards until out of Azrael's sight.

Sabaist immediately contacted two of his most trusted leaders, Chthon* and Pernicious*. Just like Sabaist, they had been with Azrael since the beginning. The three leaders quickly rounded up twenty legions each of

Sheol's fiercest soldiers. Sabaist reasoned that, to boost their odds of success, the three should divide their forces into three groups. This would allow them to cover more ground in the same amount of time. Sabaist gave the final orders: he would search the lowlands, Chthon the mountains, and Pernicious the deserts.

Day and night, the commanders and their troops scoured Callow. But day after day they searched without success. They were beginning to lose hope until one day, when Chthon was digging for food; he accidentally exposed one of the keys. Finding the key would have been cause for rejoicing, but when he tried to pick it up, he was…well, instantly vaporized! Amazingly, even after witnessing their leader vanish into thin air, others tried in vain to lift the key. They were so afraid of Azrael that they would risk the consequences of the key instead of going back empty-handed and facing his wrath. More than two hundred demons were erased by the key's mysterious power before Sabaist and Pernicious had arrived.

It did not take the two old devils long to figure out that the King had made the keys! The greatest fear of the Nether World was to come in contact with anything pure. Anything impure that touched purity would immediately die. So, the instant Sabaist understood that Deus had made the keys; he sounded a full and urgent retreat!

The two old cohorts were afraid to return to Mount

Sheol with the bad news, for they remembered their master's ill mood before leaving on their mission. They were definitely in a tough spot. For if they did not return with a good report, they knew he would hunt and execute them for sure! So, grudgingly they decided to return and take their chances.

Once back home, and after some delay, they reluctantly entered the Curule*, the central command center of the The Damned. The stronghold was the seat of evil and lay hidden, deep inside the bowels of Mount Sheol. Azrael spent most of his time there when he was not roaming throughout Terrenea. As Sabaist slinked forward, he spotted his busy master hunched over a cluttered yet orderly battle table, marking on an old tattered map. The table was blanketed with drawings, maps, scrolls, and many mysterious devices. Pernicious decided to lag back and tried to remain unnoticed.

"Your emminence." Sabaist whispered, not wanting to startle the busy ruler. "We have just returned from Callow."

The ancient devil dropped the map and quickly faced his slave in anticipation. "Yes, my minion," he answered as he slid toward the kneeling warrior. "Tell me what I want to hear!" he growled, hovering over his quivering slave.

Sabaist was bowing as low as he could and had his nose pressed onto the floor. "Your majesty, I do have good news to report! After much toil we were able to locate one of the keys!"

"Excellent...excellent, my friend. Bring it to me!" Azrael hissed, leaning closer.

"Well...ah...mm...my lord, unfortunately, we were unable to bring it back, for it held the markings of Deus himself!" Immediately, Sabaist could sense a change in the atmosphere around him. Air began rushing from the room, and he could feel a growing chill moving in around him.

"Oh merciful master, please let me explain! You must know that before we could get there, the key had destroyed two hundred of your finest warriors! I did not want to lose more of your forces, so I sounded a retreat. Please, master, if this is not pleasing to you, then I humbly beg for mercy! You know we will forever be your faithful servants! Please my lord, give us one more chance!" Sabaist remained pressed to the floor. But with the Ruler of the Damned there are no second chances.

Pernicious, hiding in the dark, tried not to breathe and remained perfectly still. The room grew cold as ice and deathly silent. Azrael seemed distracted and slowly straightened, stiff and erect. He stood motionless, grinding his teeth and staring up at the ceiling. He began to violently shake and lift his arms upward. Then, with a deafening roar, jagged streams of dark fire shot from the palms of his hands. One black flame followed another, ricocheting off the walls and ceiling, erasing the light from the room, until Curule was engulfed in absolute blackness. A massive percussion of ear-splitting sound exploded and rocked the room as the angry ruler screamed, "Curse you, wretched Deus! I will not rest until I take down you and your beloved kingdom!"

When the veil of darkness had lifted, the sulking leader stood alone amid a heaping pile of smoldering ashes. Everything and everyone in the room had been completely consumed! Still boiling with rage, Azrael shouted, "If I can't steal your keys, then I will do whatever it takes to stop your precious Terreneans from getting them."

So, the desperate ruler immediately gathered new armies in the great battle hall and commanded them to find every Terrenean boy on his quest. Every seeker must be prevented, at all costs, from getting the keys! The soldiers of evil were given orders to distract, hinder, deceive, and fight to the death if necessary. The great battle chamber resounded once again with a war cry of hate.

Azrael warned them: "Anyone who does not obey my commands will have a fate worse than that of Sabaist and Pernicious!" Fearing for their lives, the demons hurried off to take their positions.

As you can see, finding the keys is not a straightforward task for young boys. They must overcome the traps of Azrael and his army. But the King has not left them defenseless in their quest. He has given them armor for protection and the Logos for guidance. The King's armor possesses the mystifying power of the king himself. So, as long as a boy wears his armor, he is protected from the attacks of Azrael's soldiers.

Now let us rejoin my sons on the trail, somewhere near the Backbiter Mountains, as they continue their search for the keys to Sentinel's door and the esteemed Mark of the Blade.

Chapter 11

Mammon

"No one can serve two kings. Either he will hate the one and love the other, or he will be devoted to the one and despise the other. You cannot serve both the King and Money."
Logos 40:6:24

Jerol intently studied the barren mountains lining the irregular rear edge of Malevolence*. The journey had taken him two summers to find the fabled Backbiter Mountains. The mountains made of a mysterious glass-like rock. If his hunch were right, Mammon, the Desert of Greed, would lie just on the other side of the mountains' cloud-tattered ridge. Like a giant hedge, the ridge trapped the clouds and prevented them from carrying their precious rain to the other side. Encouraged that he was drawing near to where he expected to find another key, Jerol decided to push on, hoping to make the desert by nightfall. After making his way through a maze of colossal boulders, he came upon the gaping hole of a cave that disappeared back into the mountain.

On each side of the cave's mouth stood a sky-kissing wall of black glass. Jerol cautiously stepped inside the opening to investigate. He looked up and down and left and right, studying his options. He had a choice. Would he travel over the mountain's ragged surface or try to go through its heart? Going over had its advantages and disadvantages. He would have the benefit of daylight. But he would be exposed to the hungry vermin that lived on the mountainsides. On the other hand, going through the cave presented different problems. For instance, he could not tell with certainty, if the cave broke through to the other side. Perhaps the opening turned into an endless maze of tunnels. The one thing, however, that seemed most appealing was the possibility that the tight corridors might save him from another meeting with the vicious backbiters.

Backbiters*. Their name sent chills up his spine. If the legend were true, the mountains would be swarming with them. Camouflaged with black, thick, stiff bristles; these heartless rodents hide within the countless crevices that crisscross the dark mountainside. They are usually loners, but occasionally they will hunt in packs. Two thin folds of rubbery skin stretch between their front and hind legs. Their tails are slightly longer than their bodies, with sharp bristles at their ends. By using the flexible skin stretched between their legs as wings and their tails as rudders, backbiters control their free-fall from the shadows. Jumping out from the rocks, they plunge from lofty heights into steep glides and onto the backs of their unsuspecting prey. In truth, backbiters are cowards. They rarely attack from the front or from the ground, but instead choose to drop down on their prey from behind.

Once they land on a victim's back, the hungry rats will waste no time in trying to bring down their quarry by injecting paralyzing venoms through its needle-like teeth. In fact, through ages of time, Brawler tribes have trained the devilish rodents, using them as a main source of red squill, one of their most offensive poisons. Listen to me; if they ever succeed in getting you down, they will try to keep you there for days, hoping you will lose your will to fight back.

Overcrowding had forced hundreds of rats to migrate from the safety of the mountain and into Malevolence. Jerol had been harassed a couple of times on the plain, but fortunately, through quick thinking and the protection of sturdy armor, he had been able to keep from succumbing to their attacks.

Jerol had never heard of anyone ever being confronted by a backbiter in a cave. Aware of the rodent's method of attack, Jerol determined that even if the illusive rats were in the cave, the close quarters would not give them enough space to maneuver. At close quarters and slow speeds, the odds of them being seen or harmed were high. He reasoned that a backbiter would not risk a miss.

Jerol shuddered at his earlier "close calls" with the furry fiends and most definitely did not want to meet up with them again. If there were another way to get to the other side of the ridge, he was interested. So, he decided that he would take the risk and go through the cave.

Jerol stepped back out into the sunlight and pulled his oil lamp and two small pieces of flint from his belongings. He then placed the lamp on the ground and lit its wick with the sparks caused by scraping the two rocks together. With his light burning, Jerol hoisted up his heavy pack and reentered the dank cavern. From the flickering of his dim light, Jerol could see his reflection inside the dark glass walls. The reflections made him feel as if he was being followed by a large group of people. Every step he took was mirrored by the many reflections around him. As he moved deeper, to his dismay, instead of growing wider, the corridor began to narrow steadily. He was eventually forced to turn sideways while exhaling so that he could keep going! Adding more aggravation to the challenge, his light was dim and sharp pieces of rock poked out from the vice-like walls.

At one point Jerol could advance only by slowly taking a few side steps, stopping, catching his breath, exhaling, and then taking a few more steps before stopping and then starting again. But undaunted and staying true to form, Jerol stubbornly refused to become discouraged. By every appearance, he had made the best decision of hiking through the belly of the mountain because he had not seen a single backbiter. In fact, he had not seen any wildlife since entering the cave.

It was easy to lose track of time without the benefit of daylight. Not knowing whether it was day or night, Jerol continued walking until his weary legs would go no further. Reluctantly, he found a dry crevice in a nearby wall and lined its uneven surface with his cloak. He then placed his lamp and lighting stones in a spot where he could easily find them, then blew out the flame and fell fast asleep.

When Jerol awoke, he could not tell whether his eyes were open or closed, for the darkness of the cavern was thick and solid. He rubbed his eyes then felt to where he had left his lamp. Once he had light, he hurriedly chewed on pieces of sweet honeycomb, snatched his sack, and pushed ahead. Pieces of maps, clothing, and miscellaneous items were strewn about showing that many travelers had used the same pass through the mountain. This was reassuring to Jerol, for the odds looked good that if he kept moving forward, the tunnel would sooner or later work its way out of the mountain.

At long last, Jerol saw daylight in the distance. At first the glow was a small bright spot. But, it grew larger with each step he took. Finally, he pushed free of the mountain's cluthes and moved out into the welcomed sunshine. Completely unaware, Jerol had been slowly climbing uphill all the way. Tired and squinting from the prolonged lack of light, Jerol rubbed his eyes and found that he was standing on top of Beggar's Ridge! This area on the mountainside was known for harboring thieves who would attack wary strangers leaving the cave. Torn pieces of clothing were scattered across the ridge as evidence of their brutality. Luckily, this day no thieves were waiting. So, Jerol freely moved to the edge of the mountain to look into the valley below.

Anxious to scan his surroundings, Jerol would have to be patient. The passageway had been dark and regaining his sight would take some time. A familiar screech rang out from above. Even though he could not see, Jerol knew Prayer was soaring high on the steady mountain updrafts. Shielding his eyes from the blazing sky, Jerol waved to his trusted friend. Forever watching, ever-ready Prayer could always be counted on. Smiling and shifting his attention back to the arid landscape, Jerol's bleary eyes followed the narrow snaking track down the rocky ridge. Ultimately, the footpath disappeared into the dunes of a desolate lowland. As far as he could see, there was nothing but patches of needle grass, scorched thorn brush and a few brown cacti painted on a canvas of white sand. All evidence seemed to show that Jerol had reached his desired destination—the Desert of Greed*!

Chapter 12

Sea of Plethora

"Don't be lazy in whatever you do. Be enthusiastic, serving the King." Logos 45:12:11

The great expanse of desert reminded Jerol of a story he had been told as a child about a magnificent sea, once teeming with life that had been slowly transformed into a barren wasteland. Before its demise, the spectacular body of water was known as the Sea of Plethora*. Its crystal clear waters were once famed throughout Terrenea as being the purest. At midday, one could once see a gleaming white blanket of sand covering the sea's floor for as far as the eye could see.

The people who lived in the Seine* village on the shores of this pristine lake were hard working. They lived simple and fulfilling lives, thriving from the overflowing bounty of the giving waters. Day after day the village people would launch out from their peaceful shore onto the calm surface of the sparkling water to search for that day's food. The work was hard, but few came back empty-handed.

Then one day a mysterious stranger named Kleros* came from Foison*, a wealthy seafront town near the eastern side of the Backbiters, to visit their peaceful town. He was tall, dressed in the finest clothes, and wore much jewelry. Jolly and carefree, he appeared to be in need of nothing. Life was good in Seine until a few villagers became envious of the affluent stranger. They began to wonder why he never seemed to work; yet he always had plenty! In time, some began to follow him. One day he told them that if they wanted to know how they could get whatever their hearts desired, they should meet him in the town square at sunset.

Word quickly spread, and, when dusk arrived, the market square was crammed with eager villagers waiting to hear Kleros' message. The people grew silent as Kleros climbed onto a large, old stump that stood in the center of the crowd. He began to speak in a loud confident voice.

"Listen, my friends. I will not be long. If you wish to have plenty and take your ease, then listen to what I say. Tomorrow morning at sunup let each of you bring one fish and one smooth stone here to the square. The stone should be no bigger than the egg of a small flute turtle. Upon the stone mark your name. We will collect all of the stones into one container and the fish in another. Once the stones and fish have been collected, I will ask for the youngest, most capable member of the crowd to come and lift out one stone. Then I will read aloud the name written upon the stone for the crowd to hear and leave the stone here on this stump for all to see. The person whose name I read shall get to take home all of the fish contained in the other box! If each of you here tonight will bring one fish as I have asked, then the container will be filled with enough fish to last one family for a full summer! The fish can be used for food or traded for goods and services. You will not have to work for a whole summer!" And with that he walked out through the crowd and disappeared.

The people were amazed at the simplicity of his plan. "Why had they not thought of this before?" they wondered. They asked no questions and returned home for the night to think about what they had just heard.

The next morning, instead of returning to the sea as usual, most of the villagers came to see if they might get lucky and get the prize. Before the sun had even risen above the sea, an anxious, noisy crowd filled the square yet again.

In their midst sat two wooden boxes. One box was ten paces long, five paces wide and twelve hands deep. The large container was overflowing with every kind of fish. The other box was two paces long, two paces wide and four hands deep, and it overflowed with stones of different shapes and colors.

Kleros seemed to appear out of thin air and walked directly to the boxes. The people grew quiet and strained to hear what he would say. "Good morning, people of Plethora. This day will change the life of one family. I shall not tarry and will now pick from among you the one who will draw out the important stone."

He examined the crowd and spied a little girl playing in the sand at the feet of her father within the inner perimeter of the group's circle. "Child, will you please come and help me? I need you to pull out a stone from this box."

At first she was reluctant, but, after a little nudging from her parents, she decided to come forward. Every eye was glued on Kleros as he led the girl next to the box containing the multi-colored rocks. Though the street was filled with people, no one uttered a word.

"Just reach in, and, without looking, please pull out only one stone and then hand it to me," he instructed. The little girl paused to peek into the box. "Please, little one," Kleros encouraged as he gently pulled on her shoulder, "do not look into the box. Look away, reach in, and pull out one stone."

Miffed at his strict instructions, the girl looked at her mother and father, reached in, and pulled out a small, pear-shaped rock. She glared up into Kleros' face, and then slapped the angular stone firmly into his outstretched hand. "Thank you, little one," responded Kleros, choosing to ignore her obvious show of displeasure. "You may now return to your mother and father."

And with that she briskly stomped back and joined her parents. As Kleros began to speak again, the crowd's attention refocused on him.

"I hold in my hand the name of our first winner. May this be an exciting beginning for you all. The name of our first lucky winner is...Okneros*!"

The crowd let out a cheer as the winner and his family eagerly rushed forward to claim his bounty! Much celebration took place that day, and so a new way of life began for the people of Seine.

From that day forward, a new winner was chosen every seven days. The people would gather to present one person with the greatly treasured wealth. At first, life in the village carried on as usual, but after awhile, many families began to neglect the sea, risking their livelihood and eventually their trust in one another just to try to win the prize.

It did not take long before most of the town's people stopped working the sea, and instead caught only one fish a day so they could play the game. Crime began to increase throughout the once peaceful village.

The beautiful Sea of Plethora began to slowly die. Before long the sea became so overcrowded that nothing could live in it. In only a couple of summers, the beautiful sea became a cesspool of waste. Gradually, the water evaporated, leaving a barren crater of white sand. Too many people had become obsessed with the game and had not noticed that their source of survival was slowly dying right before their eyes. Eventually, the villagers were forced to abandon their town in search of food. Sadly, in the end, they lost everything they owned.

Apparently the legends were true. Jerol understood that what lay before him were the remains of that once beautiful place.

Since dusk was approaching, he decided to spend the night on the desolate ridge. It would be safer there. Prayer had already nestled down for the night in the highest branches of a weathered old tree. So, Jerol set up camp and gathered sticks and brush to fuel a meager campfire. The desert would be cold once the sun had set.

That night the sky was clear and full of a thousand shooting stars. Sitting beside the warmth of his fire, Jerol wrapped up in the soft wool of his sheepskin bed and stared up through the open sky. The sound of the crackling campfire and the sweet aroma of burning wood brought back warm memories of Palaestral. As he closed his eyes, his mind drifted back to the field where he and Prayer had shared many wonderful times. Dwelling on the peaceful days of his past, he fell sound asleep.

In the meantime, despite Jadan's desire to move forward, he had made little progress. Every time he began to make some headway, his old buddy Sin would get him in trouble and slow him down.

One defeat followed another, until Jadan became fed up. He decided that no matter what Sin did, he would march on to Mammon. He hoped that his situation would start to improve once he broke free from Malevolence. "Anyway," he thought, "I can always come back to the Plain and search another day."

One day, Jadan and Sin sat on a hilltop on the east side of Gall and stared at the silhouette of the Backbiter Mountains. The dark edge of their serrated peaks cut against the golden sky. "That is were we need to be," Jadan announced, pointing to the mountains. "Tomorrow I am leaving with or without you! Tomorrow I am starting over!" Sin, with his chin flat to the ground, let out a halfhearted grunt.

So, early the next morning, a determined Jadan with Sin still glued to his side, set out to what he hoped would be a new beginning.

Chapter 13

The Fetter

"He who owns a fetter is sure to regret it. But whoever refuses the fetter will surely be safe." Logos 20:11:15

Back on Beggar's Ridge, Jerol woke to a scorching sun and choking dry heat. His campfire had long since died leaving behind a small pile of white ashes and smoldering sticks. The once comfortable sleeping bag felt like an oven and Jerol was soaked with sweat.

He quickly propped up, peeling back the soggy covers from his chest, and then leaned back on his elbows. He rubbed the sleep and dust from his eyes and looked around. The landscape danced as waves of heat rose from the scalding sand. As the ground adjusted from the punishing heat, he could hear popping and cracking sounds.

Jerol slipped out from his bed and doused a rag in water from an animal skin flask. He rubbed the refreshing cloth across his face, neck, and arms.

As was his morning custom, Jerol spent time reading

and meditating upon the Logos, immediately followed by sending Prayer off with more notes to the King. Once he had finished his "time of reflection" and eaten his morning meal, Jerol began the long descent to the desert valley.

The land before him was mostly barren, a scene of hill after hill of rolling white sand dotted by patches of stubborn thorn bushes. "Just great," Jerol thought. "More thorns." The terrain was gritty and hot.

Even though Jerol knew he was in for another tough challenge, he had made a decision to stay on the narrow route. He had faith that there must be good reasons that the Scrolls warned about the broad way. Jerol had decided long before that he did not need to understand the Logos; his job was to obey it. Determined, Jerol trudged down the long hill and through the scorched valley.

Once Jerol reached the desert floor, the sun was directly overhead. Fortunately, his armor reflected away much of the stifling heat. To keep the sweat from blurring his view, he tied a rag across his forehead and under his helmet.

Before too long his water supply had fallen dangerously low, which forced him to shift his attention to searching for more. He knew that surface water in Mammon would be next to impossible to find. For moisture had long since evaporated with the morning dew.

Jerol would have to rely on an age-old technique he

had learned from his grandfather. He began searching for the shadiest prickle bush he could find. Before long he spotted a healthy one, about a couple hundred steps to the east.

He maneuvered around patches of ankle-high needle grass and beside the bush. About the same height as Jerol and almost forty hands wide, the plant was vibrant green—a stark contrast to its bleak surroundings. Jerol pulled out a towel from his backpack, laid the cloth on the hot sand, and slowly knelt down upon it. Next, he punched a bowl-shaped depression in the sand just beyond the outer branches of the bush, and then slid his polished sword from its leather sheath.

Perched on his knees, Jerol pushed the razor sharp point straight down through the scalding sand and worked the weapon back and forth until it was embedded halfway down its length. Jerol stood to his feet and grasped a limb of the bush. He steadied himself and stepped up on top of the hand guard. He placed one foot to either side of the handle and began jumping up and down.

With each jump the sword advanced farther down until a trickle of water leaked out from the punctured ground. Grains of sand and water began to mix and swirl, filling the hollow indentation in the ground. Prickle bushes had the special ability to store water in their root systems.

Hot, sweaty, and thirsty, Jerol patiently waited until the cool water bubbled clear before filling his flask. He quickly pulled the leather pouch to his parched lips and gulped until he could feel his body returning to life. After taking his fill, he wiped his mouth with his forearm and looked up to check the location of the sun.

By the position of the bush's shadow, Jerol determined that it was past midafternoon. He ventured back to the trail and continued to trudge ahead. The desert was beginning to cool down, which made travel not as difficult. After some time, he approached an intersection where two new paths broke off. Standing at the crossroads were weather worn signs pointing the way to the towns of Shylock and Foison, two of the richest cities of Terrenea.

The new paths were wide, mostly clear and level. Once again Jerol considered traveling on one of the wider roads. The narrow one had proved to be so difficult. Yet, instead of taking what appeared to be the easy way, he decided again to depend on the Logos as his guide.

Seeking direction, he sat down by the signs and unfurled the Scrolls. After reading for only a short while, his direction was clear—the Logos had not changed: "Broad is the road that leads to trouble" (Logos 40:7:13).

As for the narrow way, the only thing Jerol could see was a lonely track weaving over the dunes and out of sight. Disappointed, yet assured, he decided to stay on the narrow trail. And even though there was no sign to show its destination, he moved ahead.

The spirited lad was creative in entertaining himself as he walked. Sometimes he would purposefully avoid stepping on sticks or stones that were often strewn along his path. He enjoyed watching for uncommon wildlife—sand snakes, desert mice, and the extremely shy weaselfoxes. He would sometimes stop to jot down the names of birds he ran across. Typically, one would not see anything other than vultures and clouds in the sky. Often he would quietly hum and whistle melodies he had learned as a young boy.

At one point he thought he saw the distorted image of someone move over the horizon. Once the stranger was close enough, Jerol could see that the foreigner was a well-groomed, middle-aged Huckster*, from the town of Shylock*. The smiling traveler was pulling some sort of small cart on four stone wheels. The little wagon was well-built and sturdy. A colorful and ornate snakewood box was perched atop a stack of colorful quilts. The surface of the box was smooth and covered on all sides with curving patterns painted by the wood's unique and distinct grain. As the stranger drew nearer, Jerol could see what appeared to be dozens of tiny holes drilled through its sides. Unusual whistles and pops were emanating from inside the small enclosure. Jerol was cautiously curious.

"Good dee, me friend," the smiling stranger chirped, raising a hand with rings on every finger.

"Hel-lo," Jerol cautiously replied.

"Where ja headed young feller?" the friendly gent asked.

"I am on my way to Sentinel," Jerol exchanged.

"Well, pleased to meet ya! Me name is Daneion*, and what might yar name be?" the stranger asked.

"My name is Jerol."

"Listen, me gud Mr. Jerol. For many summers I have met young lads just like ye, and from what they tell me ya can expect the journey ahead to be filled with a long list of needs. Perhaps I may be of some help. I have somethin' I would like to offer ya' that has helped many a boy and will make yer travel much easier." The brazen stranger turned toward the wagon. "What I have in dis box is thee answer to questions that ye don't even know ye have!"

Jerol was curious. "Well, I must say I could use a little help now and then," he revealed.

"Ah, yes, well." The thin traveler bent over and pulled out a pair of lily-white gloves from beside the box. He slid the gloves onto his hands and slowly lifted a moving object from the box, cupping it in his hands. "Here, me good feller, is de handiest, dandiest friend that a young boy could ever have! As a matter of fact, almost every grown-up in Bravura owns at least one of these little ladies!"

Jerol watched with wonder as Daneion slowly reached out and unfurled his long fingers, revealing a beautiful, silver and grey-colored bird. Slightly taller than a sparrow, but much thinner, it had a black-tipped yellow beak and black beady eyes. The little bird just sat there grooming itself. It was well-mannered and tame.

"This, me friend, is a fetter*," the Huckster explained. "She is well trained and gentle. But listen carefully; she is not like other birds of Terrenea. She has a most amazing power. Her special ability is looked for, not only by the leaders of Bravura but by most Terreneans as well" the Huckster remarked. By this time he had Jerol's full attention.

"She has the mysterious ability to produce eggs made of pure silver! And not just one egg, me friend, but as many as yar heart desires!" Daneion claimed. "And what's more, she will produce them upon yar command!"

"You can't be serious," Jerol remarked. "That's incredible! I haven't heard of fetters before. Please, oh please, tell me more."

"Well," the Huckster continued, "so long as ya feed her the same weight of food as the eggs she lays, and ya do not tarry ta feed her shortly after she lays them, she will serve ye well. But, listen to me—If ya fail to feed her soon enough she will grow fatter!"

Jerol looked puzzled. "What?" he asked. "Did you say she would grow fatter if I didn't feed her?"

"Dat's right," Daneion replied. "I know it sounds strange, but, without the right amount of food, her body will expand instead of shrink! Ya see, if she's not fed by the passing of the full moon a weight equal to the weight of the eggs she has laid, then she will gain that amount of weight, plus a little more. This makes her terribly cumbersome and much more difficult to care for! Yes, it is a most curious thing."

Jerol was not sure he could trust this guy, but he seemed to be sincere. He studied Daneion's face. "If this is true, then let her lay for me one silver egg right now," Jerol challenged. No sooner had he spoken the words when the tiny bird sat down in the Huckster's gently cupped hands, fluttered her little wings, then stood back up revealing a beautiful, shiny, silver egg about the size of a big butter bean!

"Now do ya believe me?" piped Daneion.

Amazed, Jerol asked, "How much does she cost?"

"Oh, dat's dee best part," responded the grinning Huckster. "She's free!"

Jerol was flabbergasted. "You've got to be kidding!"

"Nope, she's all yars! Just take her," Daneion exclaimed.

Jerol's thoughts were spinning. "On the one hand, having plenty of silver would be nice! I wouldn't have to wait to get all the things I want. But, how and where would I be able to get enough food to keep the fetter satisfied? Sure, a full moon would be plenty of time to collect enough grub, but I fear that because she is so easy to use, I will wind up using more eggs than I will be able to find food for. And one more mouth to feed on the trip sure would require much extra work. What scares me even more is that I might lose my focus on the quest."

After thinking it through, Jerol responded. "Thank you, Mr. Daneion, but I'm not interested in your generous offer. Maybe some other time."

"Oh, I can certainly understand why ya might hesitate," Daneion calmly offered, pressing in closer to Jerol, "but just think of what ya would be able to buy with all of dees!" He stretched out his hand and presented Jerol with three more silver eggs! Jerol could see the reflection of his face in their polished surfaces. "Remember, dees can be traded for anything in dee whole Kingdom, anything yar heart deesires!"

Jerol turned away and began walking down the trail. He was getting annoyed with Daneion's persistence. "Thank you, but, like I said, I'm really not interested."

Jerol kept walking straight ahead. He was determined not to look back. He could not put his finger on it, but he sensed that the Huckster was not telling him the full story. Jerol knew that he had better get away as fast as he could. He would not give the stranger another opportunity to tempt him into doing something that he might later regret. As Jerol marched away, Daneion began to smile, for he knew that it was just a matter of time before they would meet again.

Chapter 14

Coveton

"Delight yourself in the King, and he will give you the desires of your heart." Logos 19:37:4

The desert was boring. Its heat was relentless and was starting to wear Jerol down. Seeking relief, he decided to travel during the cool of the night. Even though night travel was much slower than walking during the day, Jerol was willing to trade less distance traveled for a break away from the terrible heat.

Mammon at night was black as pitch and surprisingly cold. Strange, scary sounds drifted out from the darkness. Unless the moon was out, Jerol could only see as far as the meager circle of his lamplight.

One particular night, a full, and pale white moon hung low in the sky and appeared to be twice its normal size. The air was crisp and cool. Jerol stood and watched his breath rise through the moonlight as a couple of wispy clouds moved between him and the enormous glowing orb.

Off in the distance he could see a sand dune resembling a mountainous ocean wave reflecting the moon's stunning light. In hopes of getting a better vantage point from which to get his bearings, Jerol tore off on a beeline for the massive sandbank. Soon he was struggling up the dune's slippery side, sliding back one step for every two he took. Out of breath, he finally reached the top. Much to his surprise, a beautiful oasis covered the top of the dune! And he could hear faint voices coming from somewhere in the distance.

As Jerol walked on, he watched as the sandy path slowly transformed into a clean paved road constructed of round red stones. Between the dim light of his little lamp and the moonlight, Jerol could see shades of color. Trees, grass, and flowers surrounded him.

Up ahead he could see lights and noticed a dozen or so buildings resembling a town square. He continued on through an area where the streets were well lit by golden oil lanterns hanging from tall black poles. There was a tailor's shop on his left, a place to eat on his right, a blacksmith's shop, a hardware store, and even a shoe shop!

Folks were hurrying and scurrying about. The air was full of the sounds and smells of a busy marketplace. The town was strangely neat and clean. Not a speck of sand was anywhere!

Jerol rubbed his eyes. "Could this be a mirage?" he wondered. "Or perhaps a dream? I have been walking for a long time. It is nighttime. Maybe I stopped to rest and have fallen asleep. That's it," he thought. "When I open my eyes, I'll be greeting a new day."

Slowly, he pulled his hands away from his face and opened his eyes. When they focused, he could see straight ahead an elaborate sign that read, in bold golden letters, "Welcome to Coveton." Jerol knew of Coveton* as a "high class" city inhabited by wealthy Terreneans. He recalled first hearing about the town while he was living in Gelandesprung. The men were tall, handsome, and dressed in the finest of clothes. The women were attractive and dressed in expensive clothing and jewely. Jerol's attention was drawn to his left by the clip-clop of a couple of Covets, as they rode past in fancy wagons pulled by high-stepping horses. One of the gentlemen politely tipped his hat. Jerol was impressed by the fellow's friendliness.

As he walked farther down the street, Jerol happened by the window of what appeared to be a jewelry shop. The curious boy stood gazing through its main window at a fancy display of dazzling, multi-colored gems. All of a sudden, a flash of light reflecting from inside a wooden display case halted his eyes.

Jerol could not believe his eyes! The box contained a single diamond-covered key! Its size and shape closely resembled the key of Courage he had gotten back in Malevolence! Jerol's heart skipped a beat! As he pressed his face in for a closer look, a Covet* approached and whispered, "Isn't it gorgeous?"

Surprised, but not alarmed, Jerol quickly responded, "Oh, yes sir it is. Do you know if it is one of the keys to Sentinel?"

Avoiding eye contact, the stranger ignored the question and whispered back, "Listen, I can tell you're looking for a key like this. The shopkeeper isn't around so... um...just go ahead and take it. Okay? I won't tell."

Jerol was taken aback by the stranger's ridiculous suggestion. "Oh, no, I couldn't do that!" he exclaimed with a nervous laugh.

Without saying another word, the friendly gent gave a nod then disappeared into the shop. Jerol watched as the Covet switched the diamond key with three others that were made of gold! These exactly matched the appearance of Jerol's key of Courage.

"What is he up to?" Jerol wondered.

The Covet was not gone for long but returned, pointing in the window. "Well, there you go, three keys that will unlock your future. So what are you waiting for? Go ahead, take them," he prodded, leaning in closer to Jerol.

Unexpectedly, Prayer swooped down through the edge of the light, dropped a note at Jerol's feet, and then quickly vanished into the night. Prayer's sudden appearance startled them, but Jerol quickly assured the frightened Covet that there was no cause for alarm.

"Don't worry," Jerol told him. "He won't hurt you. He belongs to me."

"What a magnificent bird," the stranger remarked. He paused for a moment, placed his hand under his narrow chin, and continued. "Listen, young friend. I'll give you all three of those keys plus five diamond covered keys in exchange for the bird!" Jerol was stunned by the unexpected offer. "Well, what do you say?"

"What if those are the keys he was looking for?" Jerol wondered. Still pondering the meaning of it all, the puzzled lad bent down, picked up and unrolled the note. It read, "You shall not steal. You shall not desire anything that belongs to your neighbor. Do you not know that the wicked will not inherit the kingdom? Do not be fooled: neither thieves nor the greedy nor drunks nor those who insult others nor those who trick others will inherit the kingdom…" (Logos 4:5:19,21; 46:6:9-10).

It instantly became clear that the uneasiness that Jerol was feeling was for good reason. The glitz and glamour of the town was beginning to entice him. "I've got to remain strong," he thought to himself. "I must not listen to my feelings. I've got to stay true to the Logos."

The Covet, sensing that Jerol was becoming distracted, upped his offer again. "Listen; there are more trinkets just inside the shop door! Treasure more valuable than all those keys combined! Come on in and let me show you!"

As the Covet motioned toward the door, Jerol saw an opportunity to get away! When the Covet heard Jerol's sandals clapping on the pavement, he quickly spun around, pointed at Jerol, and began shouting in a high-pitched voice, "He's getting away! Somebody stop him!"

Instantly, the mild-mannered strangers who were casually passing Jerol on the street stopped in their tracks. The only one moving in the entire town was Jerol. About a dozen Covets focused their attention on him. People began pouring into the street from everywhere! Before long Jerol was totally surrounded.

Nervous and taken aback, Jerol was shocked that each Covet held in his hands an object that Jerol had dreamed of owning. He was surrounded by every manner of temptation: the newest games, rare card and coin collections, fine clothes, rings, and toys of every kind! The Covets were obviously followers of Azrael and were trying to distract Jerol from his mission by entangling him with covetous greed.

The ominous group tightened their circle on him like a hangman's noose. While Jerol appeared preoccupied with the impending assault, one of the Covets hurled a rank wad of lust* straight at Jerol's unprotected back! But the boy quickly drew his sword twirled and neatly divided the foul-smelling mud with one effortless motion. Half of the sticky paste tumbled past Jerol and exploded on the ground while the other half splattered across his chest, throwing him backward and off-balance. Boiling and crackling, the mysterious transparent slime quickly evaporated like steam into the chilly evening air.

No sooner had Jerol regained his footing than another attacker hurled a hatchet dipped in envy*! Jerol was not quick enough to get out of the way and was struck hard on his side. He stumbled backwards recoiling from the blow. The hatchet's blade deflected from the side of his breastplate, firmly lodging in the side of a wagon parked next to bakery shop.

Jerol was still on his feet, but a bit off balance. The Covets were reaching out and were close enough to nab him. If he were going to get away, he knew he had to act quickly! With blinding speed, Jerol swung his sword in all directions, striking every item of temptation from their hands. The accuracy and confidence of his resistance frightened the crowd, and they began backing up in retreat.

He could sense their fear and began to chase after them. One by one the sinister Covets ran away. After awhile, Jerol was the only person left standing in the middle of the street. Wielding his weapon firmly, he held the steely blade out front and looked from side to side. He then slowly backed into the shadows.

Jerol sneaked through dark alleyways to the jewelry shop where he had left his lamp. Without the lamp's light, he would not be able to travel until morning. Once back at the shop, he was relieved to find that his little light was still shining near the front door.

He scooped the lamp up, trimmed its wick with a fish bone knife, and raised the flame. The keys in the jewelry shop intrigued him, and he wanted to get a closer look. So, holding his sword at the ready, Jerol cautiously entered the shop's doorway and peeked inside. Lamplight chased the darkness from the room, leaving Jerol in shock. The entire shop was in disarray!

Numerous, grimy pieces of broken, wooden chairs and tables were lying everywhere. The inner space of the shop was laced with cobwebs stretching from ceiling to floor. "How can this be?" Jerol wondered. The shop was filthy with nothing of value inside! Its appearance did not resemble the shop's unspoiled exterior. Except for the display table and jewels next to the front window, the shop was in ruins. Upon closer inspection, Jerol discovered that the jewels and keys were brightly painted pieces of worthless wood!

The truth about Coveton had been exposed: Its buildings were elaborate fakes, designed to lure unsuspecting visitors into a sense of false security, making them easier to capture. The whole town was an elaborate ruse.

Before stepping outside Jerol wetted his finger tips and pinched out the lamp's flame. He remained alert, watching for the possible return of the Covets as he made his escape down the abandoned street.

What just a short time ago had been a bustling main street was almost silent. The only sounds were that of a creaking sign and the lonesome cry of a distant willow fox. Apparently, Jerol had passed the test. The Covet's, or whoever they were, had moved on to their next evil scam.

Jerol knew that he must get as far away from the town as possible before bedding down for the night. He did not want to risk being captured again. Luckily, on the outskirts of town, he found a lamp oil tree, refueled his lamp, and slid back into the quiet of the desert night. Though his lamp was full, he would travel by moonlight until reaching a safe distance away from Coveton.

Chapter 15

Debt

"Since he was not able to pay, the master ordered that he and his children and all that he had be sold as slaves to take care of their fetter." Logos 40:18:25

Seeking a change of scenery, Jadan hurriedly left Malevolence to search for the keys in Mammon. After several moons, he had arrived at the Backbiter Mountains. And just like Jerol, Jadan was approached by a friendly fellow and the offering of a fetter. The fellow's name was Chabal* and he was another huckster from Shylock.

Unlike Jerol, though, Jadan did not pull back, but instead held out his hand. The fetter showed no fear and hopped into the boy's outstretched hand without hesitation!

"Oh, would ya looky dar, she likes ya fur sure," Chabal observed. "Remember, don't ya forget ta feed her the same amount of food as the eggs she lays. Do this at least once every full moon."

"No problem," Jadan replied. "I have been caring for

Sin from the time he was a piglet. So, a little sweet bird will be no trouble at all."

The feisty fetter jumped from Jadan's hand and fluttered down, landing on Sin's bumpy back. Jadan was concerned that the big pig might become startled and harm the little bird. But to Jadan's delight, Sin gleefully grunted and began dancing in circles! The fetter and Sin celebrated as though they had been longtime friends.

"Well," Jadan laughed, "it looks like you two are going to get along just fine." He looked back at the smiling stranger.

"Does she have a name?" Jadan asked.

"Why yes me boy, as a matter of fact…Debt is her name," Chabal responded.

"So, how much did you say she costs?"

"Well, believe it or not, she's yars fer free!" declared the grinning huckster. "Just give her plenty of attention and remember to feed her."

"Are you kidding?" Jadan laughed. "She's free?"

"Ya, she's free."

"Well, then, it's a deal," Jadan eagerly decided.

Chabal shook Jadan's hand. "Well, I should be going, young friend. I'm late fer a very important engagement. Now don't ya forget ta feed her at the right time. It is most important."

"Tell me, what kind of food does she eat?" Jadan asked.

"Oh, dat's important ta know." Chabal reponded. "She only eats silver seed. And, she has veery strange eating habits. Be shawer not ta feed her until after she lays her eggs. Every time she gives ya an egg, ye must be sure ta feed her da same weight of silver seed as the weight of dee egg, or she will grow lazy and obese. And be careful; if ya wait too long before feeding her, she may become too much to manage."

Jadan pondered for a moment. "So, let me see if I've got it straight. I find something I want to buy. I tell the fetter how many eggs to lay. After she gives me the eggs, I feed her with silver seed."

"You've got it, me boy!" the huckster chuckled. "Now may I take my leave? I really must be going."

"Thank you very much, Mr. Chabal. May your journey be smooth," Jadan replied.

And with that, the cheerful huckster disappeared down the path leading to Shylock. Thus, for no payment on his part, Jadan gladly acquired Debt*.

Anxious to get to Coveton so he could test the fetter's worth, Jadan barked, "Come on guys, let's see if we can find those keys." So, Jadan, Sin and the fetter took off down the wide road to Coveton.

It did not take long before the fetter's beauty and charm had entranced him. Jadan was becoming more dependent on Debt with each passing day. She gave him a sense of security that he had never felt before. The more he thought about it, the more he was convinced that she would be the answer to all of his problems.

After several moons, the trio had crossed over the rugged terrain of the Backbiter Mountains, marched on the broad road through the burning sands of Mammon* and reached "the golden city". Jadan wasted no time in finding a nice place to live. Because of Debt's help he bought a three-story mansion near downtown. The excited lad was greatly relieved to be away from the gritty desert. In drastic contrast, Coveton was clean and neat. At last, no more days spent cleaning sand from his belongings.

The town seemed to possess everything Jadan had ever dreamed of. In next to no time, he became a regular fixture at the daily marketplace. Unlike his brother, who had fled from the city's temptations, Jadan completely caved in to his selfish desires. He wasted no time in using Debt's seductive power to buy anything he wanted. He lavished his home with the finest foods, clothing, armor, weapons, games, and jewelry. The list grew daily.

Just like the huckster had promised, the fetter gladly supplied all of the silver eggs that Jadan wanted. However, unaware of what was happening, Jadan was quickly becoming consumed by his out-of-control desire for stuff.

Several days passed, as did many more eggs. A couple of full moons came and went before Jadan noticed that

Debt was not looking so healthy. But, he had been so caught up in his desire for things that he had forgotten to feed her! She was starting to show signs of bloating.

By the time Jadan had made time to feed her, he could not find enough silver seed to keep her satisfied! She seemed to produce eggs faster than he could find food to feed her! Jadan did the best he could, but he just could not pull away from the marketplace long enough to properly care for her.

After a few full moons, Debt had grown greater than twice the size of Jadan! She was beginning to weigh him down. In fact, just as Chabal had warned, the fetter's demands grew to be greater than his ability to provide for them! Jadan decided that, to be rid of Debt's drag, he would have to stop using her to buy goods. So, despite his cravings, he refused to go to her for help and only traded for items with his possessions. But, because he was so far behind on collecting the food that she required, Debt continued to grow at an alarming rate!

By Jadan's estimation, she was growing at least three hands wider every day! Jadan was in a desperate situation. To feed her, he was forced to trade back every belonging he owned just to survive. In fact, to buy enough food for himself and Sin, Jadan was even forced to sell the sword and shield that his mother and I had given to him as a birthday gift.

During the next summer, Jadan barely made ends

meet! The harder he tried to catch up, the fatter Debt became! In the end, Jadan had traded all of his possessions, except for Sin, just to buy food for his growing Debt. The once beautiful bird was an ugly monster, filling the largest downstairs room of their spacious mansion. She had grown too big to fit through its door and was living in her own filth!

Jadan considered abandoning the needy fetter, but Kingdom law restricted him from getting rid of Debt until he successfully caused her to shrink to her original size. The trick, of course, was feeding her the right amount of silver seed at the right time. Debt could not be blamed for Jadan's dreadful situation. Instead, it was his mismanagement and abuse of her that had done him in.

Eventually, because of her enormous size, Jadan was compelled to give up his grand home and move to Dire Straights, a community near the outskirts of Coveton. In Dire Straights boys and girls lived with their sick fetters. Some birds were as big as barns! Every type of people—of all ages and backgrounds—lived in Dire Straights, but one thing everyone had in common was bondage to their fetters' enormous appetites.

While living in Dire Straights, Jadan had to take on various jobs just to survive. He worked for a blacksmith as an apprentice, shoeing horses. He toiled as a lantern lighter, responsible for keeping Coveton's street lanterns lit each night. He worked as a baker's assistant, and then landed a job in the jewelry shop where he learned how to make an honest trade for honest pay. For once, Jadan was starting to get it right.

It took working every single day for two summers, from before sunrise to well past sunset and without a break, before Jadan had gotten Debt back down to her original size! She had taken everything he had except Sin. Amazingly, Jadan had never neglected Sin during his entire ordeal with Debt, for Sin had always been an integral part of Jadan's daily life.

So, with Debt back down to her original size, Jadan could return her to her original owner. He was so anxious to get rid of her that he could not wait until morning to leave. So, he hurriedly crammed some clothes in an old burlap sack and left in the middle of the night. He had to travel an entire season from Coveton

to Shylock, because the wealthy village was nestled in the foothills of the northern slopes of the Mirth. Finally, after many harrowing days, Jadan, Debt and Sin found their way back across the scalding wasteland. Once in Shylock, Jadan wasted no time in beginning his search for the fetter's old home. He would not rest until he was rid of her.

It was midmorning before Jadan had found Chabal's place. He hadn't changed a bit. Even though surprised by the unexpected visit, the old huckster was glad to see Debt and welcomed her back home. But, before Jadan could get away, Chabal tried his best to give her back.

"Ya know, its good ta see me fetter again, but she really needs ta live elsewhere. Won't ya take har back? I'll give ya a better deal dis time! In fact, I'll give ya two fetters. Dat way ye can use one ta buy food for da other!" Chabal persuaded.

Jadan rolled his eyes. "Listen, Mr. Chabal. I've had enough of Debt. I wouldn't wish her on anyone else! I lost everything I owned because of her. I almost lost myself. I'm done with Debt!" Jadan walked away with a smile. He felt like a brand new person. "I will never own another fetter as long I live!" Jadan vowed.

Jadan and Sin returned home to Coveton. He slowly began rebuilding his life. But, even though he had gotten rid of Debt, his desire for things and toys remained a driving force inside him. "I have done without so much for so long, I deserve to buy myself something that will make me feel better!" Jadan often thought to himself.

Once again his happiness depended on possessions instead of serving the King! Jadan would spend hours, even days, negotiating for something that he wanted. He would not quit until his thirst for comfort was quenched.

The Coveton's were patient in setting their trap for Jadan. As long as he was playing their game, they would keep up appearances. Pretending was easy. Azrael's order was to detain the boys at all costs. And he was supplying them with all of the props they wanted. So, if it took them many summers to capture Jadan, then they were willing to wait.

Still blinded by his lust for things, Jadan was unable to see how old and rundown the town was. It took living in Coveton for another summer before he understood that, even though he had worked hard and was rich again, he was yet empty on the inside.

One evening, after a particularly long day, Jadan was walking home from work. As he passed by the shoe shop his eyes were drawn to the image of someone he thought he knew in the reflector of a nearby street lantern. The light was hanging on a porch post just outside the steps to the shop. He halted in mid-stride and looked back up the street, but no one was there!

As he drew closer to the shiny oval tin, he was stunned

when he realized the likeness was his reflection! Suddenly, his eyes were opened. He was just like those buildings on Main Street. They looked so pleasing on the outside, but on the inside they were really empty and rundown! Not typical for Jadan, a passage from the Scrolls ran through his mind, "Woe to you, you hypocrites! You are like whitewashed tombs, which look beautiful on the outside, but on the inside are full of dead men's bones and everything unclean" (Logos 40:23:26). He knew right then and there, that he had wasted too much of his life!

Reacting to the revelation, Jadan became restless and began searching for a way out of Coveton. "If I'm ever going to get to Sentinel, I better get back to hunting seriously for those keys. The question is, should I stay here and continue to look for them or should I go back to Malevolence? Maybe I would have better success if I went back to the plains," he thought. "At least I know my way around there." But Jadan never felt confident that going back was the answer. Several more days passed as he struggled to decide what he should do.

Jadan told no one of his plans. As far as the town's people knew, Jadan was close to belonging to them.

One day Jadan was daydreaming, sitting on the floor, and leaning back to back with Sin. The lazy pig was lying on his side and peacefully snoozing.

Jadan spoke out loud. "Maybe Euphoria is where

it's all going to come together; maybe all four of the keys are there." Barely aroused by Jadan's comment, Sin remained motionless except for partly raising one ear, then letting out a halfhearted grunt.

Over the last few days Jadan had been telling Sin stories about a new place called Euphoria Peak. He had learned about the enchanted mountain during a casual conversation with the townspeople. They told him that if one were willing to risk the long journey there, his wildest dreams might come true.

Well, Sin had no interest in Jadan's new idea. He had heard it all before. The only thing he wanted to do was lie around and dream of honey-drenched acorns and wallowing in the mud. So, Sin simply ignored Jadan's comment. But after living with Sin for so long, Jadan had learned to accept the pig's lack of enthusiasm.

So, Jadan resolved to look forward with a hopeful heart and not let disappointment rule. He had gathered enough confidence to continue on despite Sin's indifference. One day, Jadan dusted off his clothes and set out to find "the enchanted mountain of pleasure" which just maybe, this time would turn his luck around.

Chapter 16

Euphoria

"A fool finds pleasure in evil conduct, but a man of understanding delights in wisdom."
Logos 20:10:23

The long string of mountains was a welcome sight, spreading out before Jerol from one end of the horizon to the other. The tallest and most famous of Mirth's snow covered peaks, Euphoria* stood in silent beauty before a pale grey sky. At its base were spacious grassy fields running up long inclines through pine groves of green. The pinewood forest wove up the mountainside until giving way to many empty, jagged, rocky cliffs and ledges.

Jerol walked over to a flat, waist-high rock and sat down. His eyes tracked up the slopes along uneven ridges to the higher elevations blanketed with white snow that was sparkling in the sunlight. Detail on the tallest point of the mountain was hard to make out, for a sheet of wispy white clouds was blocking his view.

Jerol dug into his pack and retrieved his looking glass

and continued to trace the narrow path. He followed its winding line through the foothills and along the mountain's side until the thin track vanished into the chalky haze. Back down the slope, Jerol noticed a narrow column of smoke drifting up and spreading out high above the timberline. He followed the wavy column of smoke down to a spot near the upper rim of the foothills.

"Must be a camp up there," he thought, "and, if there's a camp, that means someone or something is living in those hills!"

The footpath going up and through the pine grove seemed to be the best path through the mountain, but Jerol did not want to run across unfriendly strangers. He had two choices: take the mountain line through the pine grove and possibly be attacked by whatever was making the smoke, or move off the trail and risk getting lost. Jerol decided once again to stay on the narrow way and cross through the pines.

It was the Season of Birth and the midmorning hillside was dancing in a kaleidoscope of colors. The air was full with the sounds of buzzing bees feeding on the morning flowers and a flock of singing songbirds passing overhead. After walking through a long patch of knee high daisies, Jerol entered the evergreen thicket near the mountain's base. The path was carpeted with pine needles and twisted uphill through line after line of old, lofty pine trunks gently swaying in the steady mountain breeze. The air was full with the crisp, clean scent of pinesap. In a little while, he began to hear what sounded like muffled music riding the breeze from somewhere deep inside the forest. "It might be the wind playing tricks," he thought. He did not let the sound scare him and decided to keep moving forward.

But, the deeper through the woods he advanced, the louder the racket became. As he drew closer the noise began to take on patterns and pitch. He began to recognize a melody. He was sure; the sound was definitely music. Unable to pinpoint the source, he stopped to get a better sense of the music's direction and then moved toward it. In a strange way, the playful harmonies reminded him of his boyhood days in Palaestral and Agog. He would occasionally glimpse the smoke column through the numerous needle-fanned limbs of the old pines. He appeared to be getting closer to the smoke's origin. And the music was coming from the same direction.

"Why is this enchanting music coming from such an isolated place? What does it mean?" he wondered. Jerol searched until mid afternoon, until coming to the edge of a clearing and an open field of waist-high grass. The music was drifting across the field from the other side of a row of young pines, which were partly hidden by a cover of thick underbrush. Jerol could see the belching column of greyish black smoke rising from just behind the bushes. He pondered, "Should I pass by or should I investigate? If the strangers are friendly, perhaps I can restock my supplies. The music sounds safe enough. But what if I'm wrong; it could mean disaster." Curiosity sometimes could be a ill-behaved companion on the road. "What *is* on the other side of those trees?" he wondered. Deciding to take the risk, Jerol cautiously moved through the grass and across the field to try to untangle the mystery.

Chapter 17

The Lyrics

"The clerics took their position, as did the Lyrics, with the musical instruments with which they praised the King and sang." Logos 14:7:6

Jerol quietly crawled through the gnarly patch of underbrush being careful to get noticed. Before long, the thicket opened into a wide clearing where, through a stand of wild willow weeds, he spotted five square, grass huts surrounding a roaring campfire. Smoke was billowing skyward and out of the forest. An inner ring of smooth stones and outer loop of green turtle shells that were about ankle high enclosed the fire. Holding hands, singing loudly, and dancing in a circle around the bouncing flames were seven slender and graceful figures. On one side sat a group of twelve musicians playing various instruments that Jerol had never seen before. And surrounding them all was a crowd of families, young and old, watching and singing along.

Jerol slowly crouched low at the clearing's edge, peeking through gaps between the shafts of the tall plants.

He stood still and listened intently. "A mighty stronghold is our King, Our Protector never failing; Our helper He among the flood of Terrenean's trials prevailing..." Jerol was not positive, but from the words they sang, he thought the singers and dancers might be part of the beloved Lyric* tribe.

The Lyric people were incredibly gifted in the language of music and famed for their skillful "praise giving," the special craft of exalting King Deus. One thing that Deus loved was the praise of his followers. But, most Terreneans were more naturally inclined to self-praise. Giving praise to others required much practice and effort. So, praising the King was a learned skill.

Legend taught that these serious, yet joyful, poets had been alive since the beginning of Terrenea and were a chosen tribe. The King had selected them to be special leaders who would teach the nation about himself and his Kingdom of Light through the language of music and dance.

However, for hundreds of summers Azrael had been able to deceive many of the Lyrics' most gifted singers and musicians. Through constant temptation and promises of fame and fortune, the evil lord had lured more of them to serve him than King Deus! This sorrowful band of souls came to be known as the Preeners*.

Preeners usually dressed in colorful clothes. Their girls and women wore many pieces of dazzling jewelry, and applied bright paint on their faces and lips and around their eyes. Some had even carved their bodies with knives changing their appearance in the quest for perfection. Many Preeners wore ear and nose rings, tattoos, and other kinds of body paint. Now, these types of effects were not bad or wrong, but the Preeners used them for drawing attention to themselves. Various male Preeners would spend days lifting and moving heavy rocks, making their bodies appear more muscular than the average Terrenean man. They valued outward appearance over inward character. The Preeners were mostly known, however, for abusing Deus's gift of music. They were experts at praising anything except the King!

You see one of Azrael's most important plans is to influence people by misusing the power of music. Putting his message into forms that the people are already familiar with has proved to be most effective. Music is another powerful tool that he uses to spread his religion of Hedonism, the twisted doctrine of pursuing pleasure above everything else.

But, The Logos teaches that pleasure may be bad or good. The person's motive in seeking gratification determines its value. Behavior from good motives will produce healthy pleasure. But, seeking pleasure over service of the King produces harmful results.

While the crowd was preoccupied with the celebration, a younger participant noticed Jerol hiding among the reeds. Jerol froze hoping the boy had not spotted him. But, Jerol watched in fear as the lad began nudging those around him, pointing in his direction. They began smiling and nodding, motioning him over. Jerol was not sure what he should do. If he ran, surely they would track him down. He decided to explain who he was and where he was headed. So, Jerol cautiously stood up and stepped out and into the open. Almost immediately, the dancers and musicians stopped! The village grew silent. Every eye turned to look at the stranger who had just entered their camp. To Jerol's amazement, the child who had first spied him, took him by the hand, and led him back to where the child had been seated. Because of that, the dancers and crowd resumed the celebration as though nothing had happened. One by one each villager welcomed Jerol and invited him to sit by the fire, to join in as they sang of the King's kindness, love, majesty, and provision.

Jerol had wandered into the village of Melodia*, inhabited by a group known as Psalmists*. This sect of the Lyrics had not fallen for the dreadful Ruler's tricks and was carrying on the tradition of the King. Though ordinary in appearance, their lives were dedicated to sharing the knowledge of righteous praise giving with whomever would listen.

Very relieved, Jerol watched and listened as, with great joy and enthusiasm, the Psalmists danced and sang. Never had he seen such an honest display of affection for the King.

Jerol thought, "Today I have seen what it means to truly honor my King. They use not only their voices to praise him, but their bodies as well. They hold nothing back. I must learn from these fine people and take their devotion and passion with me on to Sentinel." Jerol stayed for the rest of that day celebrating with and learning from his new friends. They fed him like royalty and let him camp that night in safety by the warmth of their fire.

The next morning Jerol awoke and continued fellowshipping with them. He eagerly asked many questions about their gifts. Then about midafternoon he decided to get back to work. He still had three more keys to find. So, he reluctantly told his new friends that he had greatly enjoyed their company, and was grateful for everything they had done for him, but that he needed to move on.

Before leaving their village, a few of the elders came to Jerol with a warning. They explained that Preeners lived on the mountain where he was headed and would be disguised as Psalmists.

"But, how will I know if it's you or them?" Jerol asked.

The chief elder explained, "The difference will be in the words they sing and how they dance. If the words do not reflect the teachings of the Logos, then they are not of us. Beware, young lad, for they are cunning and have ways of planting evil seeds within your heart. If you allow those seeds to get inside, they can grow into a tangle of wicked weeds, which will choke out the fruit of the Scroll's teachings! You must remember, my child. Never forget!"

"I will not forget." Jerol responded with confidence. He then embraced and thanked each of them for their hospitality and concern. The elders and village began to clap as Jerol turned to leave. After double-checking his pack, he called for Prayer, waved to the crowd and made his way back to the winding trail. He was not sure what to expect from the days ahead, but he knew that he was ready for the challenge.

Chapter 18

Bacchus

"You will never be faced with a temptation that is not already common to Mankind. The King promises to never let you be tempted beyond what you can handle. Always take heart, when temptations come, for the King will provide you with a way out." Logos 46:10:13

Even though Jerol had stayed only a short time with the Psalmists, his visit had been a life-changing experience. Their complete devotion to the King was inspiring. Jerol felt invincible and departed their camp with a renewed sense of dedication to the Crossing.

Jerol continued his climb to the top of Euphoria. He took the Psalmist's warning seriously and stayed alert, watching for signs of Preeners. He traveled on for several days without a major incident. A bad headache was the only thing giving him trouble. Not long after leaving the Psalmists' camp, his head had started throbbing with a dull, annoying ache. He passed the pain off as due to the drastic change in elevation. He ignored the aggravation and kept pushing higher up the incline.

Finally, he reached the border of the snow-capped part of the mountaintop. The beauty of the wintry scene took his breath away! The landscape was difficult to describe, dotted with evergreens rising up through rocks enclosed in rolling drifts of pearly white snow. The sky was grey and calm.

As Jerol stood soaking in the view, a bead of sweat rolled down his brow and came to rest at the corner of his eye. When he reached up to wipe the drop away, he noticed that the air felt abnormally warm

"This is strange," he thought. "It's much too warm for snow. What's going on? The snow should be melting." He looked all around but could not find any signs of thawing.

As he stood scratching his head, he saw a blackbird fly by and slam against the side of a large boulder! The stiffened little bird tumbled to the ground leaving behind a column of floating feathers.

Then, he spotted a young doe off in the distance beyond the bird. She was jumping up and down in the same spot, spinning and stumbling in circles. The scene was a most troubling sight!

Jerol knelt down and scooped up a handful of snow. To his bewilderment, the material was not even cold! The fine dust looked and felt like the talcum powder his mother had often used on him as an infant. Jerol suspected that the white stuff was Alabaster. It looked as if Azrael had been working overtime, for the whole mountaintop was covered in it!

Alabaster was a white powder that possessed the mind-bending power to change one's perception of reality. Inhaling only a few particles of the evil dust would cause a person to feel and act abnormally. While under the influence of the dust's power, the person's ability to make smart decisions would be greatly compromised. Because the dust would cause a person to feel intense pleasure its affect was extremely dangerous. Craving its promise of happiness, many Terreneans would inhale the dust on purpose, not caring that they would put themselves and others at great risk of harm or even death. Once under the control of Alabaster, you would be totally unaware of where you were or what you were doing. This was a deadly combination.

"That must be it," Jerol thought. "The bird, the deer, my pounding head. It all adds up."

Jerol quickly yanked a handkerchief from his knapsack. He doused the thin cloth in water, and firmly sealed off his mouth and nose, and began walking up the rocky grade. "Not too fast!" he cautioned. "I don't need to stir up more of this dust."

After trudging for several hundred more steps, Jerol had climbed to the upper ridge where the air was much colder. He continued through a patch of thick fog that was hovering low to the ground. Fortunately, the time was midday, and he could see well enough to keep going. He was determined to not stop until he had walked out of danger. But, seeing Prayer was becoming more difficult because of the heavy mist.

Even though the sun was straight overhead, it was cold enough that he had to wrap up in his woolen cloak. By the feel of the cold mountain air, Jerol figured he must have been nearing the crest of the mountain. At last he felt assured that he had gotten far enough away from the dangerous powder. So, he uncovered his face and took in a deep breath from the clean mountain air! Stopping to rest, Jerol looked up the rise to see how close he was to the summit.

Off in the distance and through the haze, Jerol could faintly see the outlines of what looked like a small cart and a short stocky person standing before a dark rocky wall. As he hiked closer, he noticed that the cart was made of a rough wooden box sitting atop two rusty-spoked, waist-high wheels and one leg for a prop. The wagon resembled a square wheelbarrow with two handles extending parallel to the ground. The box was filled with bottles and containers of many sizes, shapes, and colors.

Jerol was not in the habit of talking to strangers and did not look up as he passed by. However, as he moved past the cart, the little guy began to wave, trying to get his attention. "Greetings! Greetings, good sir!"

Not wanting to be rude, Jerol stopped and turned around. "Good day," Jerol nodded.

"Pardon my curiosity," the stranger remarked, "but I noticed as you were walking toward me that you were holding your head as though in some kind of pain."

Jerol raised a hand to his brow, "Well, that's very kind of you to ask. I do have a bad headache," he responded.

"Well, someone must be watching out for you, because you've come to the right place!" exclaimed the friendly gent pointing to his wagon. "You're in luck, I have loads of treats on my cart that are for such aches and pains."

Jerol did not know it, but the harmless looking fellow belonged to the dangerous Opiate group! His name was Bacchus*, and he was one of the band's most cunning leaders.

The Opiates* were evil gypsies, followers of Azrael, who worked in disguise on the mountains of Callow and Bravura. They spent day and night setting traps of addiction*, hiding them in the most unexpected places. Once caught, an unsuspecting victim would have a difficult time choosing service instead of pleasure, which in turn would lead to unhealthy consequences. Sometimes the sweet-tasting poisons would even lead to death!

Jerol rummaged through the bottles and boxes on Bacchus' colorful cart. "Sir," Jerol commented, "I don't think that I'm familiar with these medicines. Thanks for your generous offer, but I'm really in a hurry and need to move on."

Bacchus perceived that Jerol's pain was getting worse, and quickly pushed a bottle into his hand. "Oh, don't worry, my boy. Just hold your breath, drink this down, and you'll feel better in no time," he instructed.

Jerol brought the murky brown bottle up to his face for a closer look. He could not figure out what the bottle contained, and the tag did not offer much insight. The label was badly stained and weathered with the word "Spirits*" inked across its top.

While he studied the faded label, a group of six boys lumbered out of the fog and down the path toward him. One was stumbling. All were laughing loudly. Two spoke with slurred speech and were hard to understand.

Bacchus explained to Jerol that the young boys were just like him, for they were on their way to Sentinel. Jerol asked them how long they had been on Euphoria. The boy who had been stumbling, a small boy with glazed-over eyes, just looked at him with an empty stare. Another older-looking guy with bloodshot eyes and beard-covered face said he'd been living with some Preeners for so many summers that he had lost count. The others shared that they had been there for at least the last four or five summers.

Jerol felt a shooting pain dart through his head. The

boys began to urge him to take a drink.

"Go ahead—try the Spirits," the older boy pushed. "They won't hurt you."

"Yeah, I used to have all kinds of problems until I started using the Spirits," volunteered another boy.

"Uh-huh, me, too. Now, I can't start my day without a drink or two. It really gets me going," piped up another.

The constant throbbing had become almost unbearable, and the promise of relief was starting to make the little brown bottle look much less threatening. Getting rid of his pain sounded tempting, but deep in his soul he did not have peace about the Spirits. "But, I'm outnumbered and afraid that I will insult them if I don't go along with them. It has been such a long time since I've been around other guys. It would be great to be part of a group again." Jerol knew he should go, but he was tired. Another strong ache pounded in his head. He studied for a moment, then lifted the bottle up and…

Chapter 19

Sunstones

"You traitors, don't you know that friendship with the Preeners' world is hatred toward the King? Anyone who chooses to do what the Preeners do becomes an enemy of the King."
Logos 59:4:4

Meanwhile, the straightness and ease of travel on the wide road, combined with his stubborn pride, had driven Jadan to brave the unknown and travel on to Mirth*. Though, not long after arriving at the mountain's base, he happened upon Sophistdale*, a large village of Preeners.

As a matter of fact, he had been living in the village for the last couple of full moons. During that time, the Preeners daily filled his mind with doubt about the way of life taught by Deus and the Scrolls. Instead, they had been encouraging him to "do it if it feels good" and to ignore the Logos.

The villagers of Sophistdale had been resourceful in spreading Azrael's music everywhere throughout

Terrenea, but the half-truths were having their most devastating affect on the young folks of Agog and Gelandesprung. To some youth, the Preeners' music had become like a popular religion. They worshipped the singer and the sound. Without even realizing it, kids were filling their minds with messages of "I don't need anyone else but me," "I want it now and I'm not going to wait for it," and "As long as it doesn't hurt anyone else, I'm gonna do it." Regrettably, they were ignoring the Way of the Light, the only true worship acceptable to the King. The Way's focus was on maintaining a friendship with Lord Deus. To trust in his promises and do what makes him happy instead of following your feelings. Well, Jadan, not unlike many other kids his age was unconcerned with what the King thought and loved the Preeners' music.

Besides Jadan's love of their music was his fascination with sunstones*, amazing hobby rocks owned by almost every Terrenean family.

Sunstones were made from rectangular slabs of gemstone in different sizes and thicknesses. Most sunstones were leaned upon a wall in the Preener's home. Even more fascinating was the way in which the crystals worked.

At the owner's command, they would fill with dancing images of colorful lights! These moving lights would show scenes from other locations in Terrenea.

Every day throughout Mankind, folks could be found reclining in their homes, staring into their stone's glowing sides for long periods of time. Sunstone-watching was especially popular in the evenings, and typically lasted from sundown until bedtime.

Well, sunstones were nothing new for Jadan. We had one in our home when he was a child. In fact, almost every home in Terrenea had at least one. In the beginning, the magical stones were used by Terrenea to inform, to share helpful information, to encourage, and to warn. They usually contained information, which was entertaining, informative or influential, or sometimes even a combination of the three. If there was something important that needed to be shared with all of the people, these crystalline rocks were the main tools used to get the job done. But, the way the Preeners used them was different than Jadan had ever seen before.

One day he was visiting with Dirge*, one of his new Preener friends. Dirge led him into the family room where he lit up a large sunstone. The slab was one of the widest Jadan had ever seen. Instantly, the glass-like rock filled with disturbing pictures showing one Terrenean murdering another! Jadan had never seen anything like it before and felt uncomfortable. Even so, curiosity kept his eyes glued to the stone.

After awhile, Dirge apparently became bored of watching the fighting and changed the crystal to another scene showing Preeners shouting and cursing! Still not satisfied, Dirge switched the picture again to images that were so shameful that I cannot even speak about them! Jadan spun his head away, but he continued to watch out of the corner of his eye.

Surprised and embarrassed, he began to ask Dirge about the meaning of what they were seeing. "What are you doing? These can't be the sorts of things we should be watching!"

Dirge snickered. "Listen friend, don't get yourself all twisted up in a knot. These stories are what our leader calls entertainment, and daily entertainment is every Preener's right. In fact, it is our favorite pastime. Recreation is vital to our survival. It helps us to relax, and, you know, recharge. Most of what you were seeing was only pretend. So, what's the big deal?"

Well, as usual, Dirge was only half right. Entertainment is not always bad. In fact, King Deus requires that Terreneans periodically rest. Many find entertainment to be a great aid in their pursuit of relaxation. However, the kind of entertainment Dirge was trying to offer, even though make-believe, was full of Azrael's harmful underlying messages. Dirge's life was out of balance and unhealthy.

Once a sunstone had enticed you, turning away would be most difficult. In reality most of the stories shown in the glowing rocks were another part of Azrael's plan of spreading his message. He was using them as tools to slowly convince Mankind that entertainment was just as important as service. If he could get Terrenea wrapped up in entertainment, he could prevent them from serving the King.

Gradually over time, just as he had done with music, Azrael had gained influence over most of the folks who determined what was displyed in the crystals. This allowed him to infect the land on a grand scale with his self-serving religion.

Jadan had never been disciplined in applying the principles of the Logos. Without the stability they offered, he was easily fooled by the grand deceiver's tricks. At first, Jadan was embarrassed by most of what he saw. But as more time passed, he began to grow accustomed to the images inside the amazing stones and to think that watching them was not so bad! And, as you may have already guessed, he was even beginning to practice the dark religion of Hedonism, instead of following the King.

Always looking for new ways to abuse familiar things, Azrael had long ago come up with another clever idea for misusing the stones. He affectionately named his new diversion Dancing Lights. Dancing Lights* was another popular activity with kids throughout Callow. The game allowed the viewer to interact with the bouncing pictures in the sunstones. Through the use of a baffling contraption called a stickbox, the observer was in complete control of the images.

To most the games were fun and harmless. Many youngsters would play the games for only a reasonable amount of time and stop without any harm being done. But many would sit entranced, in front of the flickering lights for long periods of time. Something about the games demanded so much of their attention that they could hardly think or do anything else. Azrael seized every opportunity to keep young Terrenean's minds tied up in light games, robbing Deus and Terrenea of much of the youth's usefulness!

As you have learned, Jadan had a personality that usually sent him head first into anything he enjoyed. So, before long he was spending too much time with Dancing Lights. The rush of fun planted its hooks in him and, just like his Preener friends, he was choosing to stay inside more and more on beautiful days, glued to the floor in front of imaginary scenes instead of playing outside in a world of wonder. Something was definitely out of kilter in Jadan's life. Loving to play light games did not make him a bad person. But, his passion kept him from having the healthy balance of life's lessons that would produce the skills needed by every warrior in Sentinel.

Jadan plunged his senses daily into the world of the Preeners. He began to feel as though he were trapped in a whirlwind, for no matter how hard he tried, he could not get out! In the end, he became so exhausted that he collapsed. The Preeners called the condition “burnout”.

Depressed and disillusioned, Jadan recognized the same empty feelings he had felt back in Coveton. “Here we go again,” he thought. “There must be more to life than this,” he told Sin. “We’ve got to get out of here before it’s too late!”

So, one day Jadan did again what he had always done. He did not plan. He did not think. He just filled up his traveling sack and moved out.

With Jadan, not much was for certain, but this was one time when he seemed to be single minded. So, with Sin still tagging along, Jadan charted a new course and set out for Euphoria, the highest point in all of Terrenea. After feeling so low, he wanted only one thing: to get as high as possible!

Chapter 20

Spirits

"Do not get drunk, which leads to poor decisions. Instead, be filled with the Logos."
Logos 49:5:18

After a couple of days, just after first light, Jadan and Sin were walking near a place on the mountainside where the wide and narrow trails ran to within about fifty steps of each other. In uncharacteristic manner, Jadan wondered whether he should try the narrow way for a change.

"So far, the wide road hasn't worked out so well," he reasoned out loud. "I wonder, if we tried that little path over there, if we might get lucky and meet up with Jerol. It would be great to see him again. Sometimes I really miss him. He was always so level-headed. I'd never tell him, but I kind of miss all of that free advice I never asked for. Hey, come to think of it, not one good thing has come from taking the wide road. So, Mr. Sin, what have we got to lose?" Jadan paused for a moment. "Come on, boy. Let's try something new."

With Sin following close behind, Jadan crossed over and started moving up the mountainside. The track weaved its way up through a field of flowers, a beautiful evergreen forest and disappeared into the snow-covered hills. The morning was going well until Jadan jammed his big toe on a rock hidden beneath the snow.

"Woeoooo!" Jadan shouted, stumbling and falling down onto his hands and knees. When he pulled up his throbbing toe to see how badly he hurt it, he happened to notice another set of footprints in the snow just a few paces away. Steady winds had blown loose snow from the trail and had revealed the shallow impressions. They dotted the snow in a fairly straight line and as far as Jadan could see. His heart leapt with excitement!

"Could these belong to Jerol?" he wondered. "They sure look like his size."

When he knelt down to get a closer look, Jadan felt a peculiar and steady pressure on the back of his eyes. But, because he was so excited by the possibility of finding his brother, he did not pay much attention to it. Instead, he continued looking at the prints a little more closely.

While Jadan was busy with his investigation, Sin got bored and decided to go exploring. He did not get far before running across a hill made entirely of snow. One of Sin's prized activities was wallowing. It really did not matter what he rolled in, as long as he could get completely covered with it.

Sin made a beeline for the mountain of white, leapt through the air, dove headfirst and disappeared into the heaping mound, sending a cloud of white blowing out in every direction. All was quiet. Sin had vanished.

Well, before long the swine's squealing, tossing, rolling, and flipping shattered the stillness of the hillside! The frenzy continued until he collapsed from exhaustion; after awhile, he rejoined Jadan back on the trail. Jadan could not believe his eyes! Sin was completely painted in white from head to tail and hardly recognizable. The edgy pig looked as though someone had plopped him down in a huge tub of honey and rolled him in a sack of flour!

Jadan began laughing hysterically! Sin spun in circles, stumbling over snow-hidden rocks and flipping sideways, and then landed in a spread-eagled heap. The hyper pig did not stay down long, however, and sprung back up onto his feet. He began darting back and forth across the trail, throwing his head back and pointing his snout straight up, blowing out puffs of white and squealing. Jadan watched in wonder as the snorting snowball darted away, fading into the white of the mountainside.

Jadan was uncharacteristically patient and waited nearly one half of a day for his buddy to return. Five times he called out for Sin, but he could only hear his own voice echoing back.

Since Sin never responded, Jadan decided that his pig must have not been returning. It was the middle of the day and important time was wasting. He wanted to find Jerol before sunset; he was anxious to see his brother again. The footprints looked fairly new, and, if they belonged to Jerol, he was probably not far away! So, for the first time ever, Jadan moved on without his favorite sidekick.

In an odd sort of way, the footprints had most likely saved Jadan's life, for they had kept him focused on his brother. If he had allowed curiosity to lure him off the path, he most likely would have become overcome by Alabaster and not have come back!

So, with a great sense of urgency, he moved on. After a while, the annoying pressure behind his eyes began to get stronger and creep deeper inside his head. His skull felt as though it were caught in a vice that was gradually tightening with each step he took. The pain had grown to be so distracting that he did not even notice that his brother was only a hundred steps away!

Jerol was still in intense conversation with the group of wayward boys. They stood around thirty steps away from Bacchus, who was fiddling with the bottles on his cart and mostly obscured from view by the heavy fog. Bacchus spotted Jadan coming up the path and motioned him over.

As Jadan came near, the sly gypsy offered him a bottle

of the same beverage that he had already given to Jerol. "Looks like you could use a break, young fella," he beckoned with an extended arm. "Here, try some of my delicious sweet tea. It's guaranteed to cure what ails you."

Well, Jadan was known to be many things, but cautious was not one of them. He had worked up a big thirst, and his head was pounding. The cold, refreshing drink looked awfully inviting. So, throwing caution to the wind, he snatched the bottle, chugged the liquid down, handed the bottle back to Bacchus, and wiped his mouth on his forearm.

Bacchus urged him to sit down and relax. He assured Jadan that he would start to feel better in a jiffy. Jadan politely thanked him for the swig and began walking away.

Jerol heard his brother's voice and wedged his way out from the crowd. "Jadan, is that you?" he shouted. "When did you get here?" Hearing his brother's voice snapped him back to his senses. Fortunately, Jerol had not tried the mysterious elixir, though he still held the container in his hand.

Jadan and Jerol ran to each other and briefly embraced. They laughed and exchanged questions and answers, each talking at the same time. Jadan saw the bottle in his brother's hand and told Jerol about how amazing the tonic was, and that his headache was almost gone.

Jerol became concerned and glanced over at Bacchus, who was still standing by the cart and trying to look uninterested. Jerol could see a sinister smile stretched across his weathered face. Even though Jadan seemed to be fine, Jerol still felt leery of the situation.

We had taught our sons not to eat or drink anything offered to them unless the stuff was from another trusted relative, a trusted healer, or us. In Jerol's estimation, the smooth-talking stranger was far from matching those descriptions!

Bacchus could see the distrust in Jerol's body language. "Come on, young fella. Don't look so worried." The clever salesman pointed to Jadan as he moved toward Jerol. "Look, your brother's doing great. Does he look like someone who's worried?"

While Jerol focused on the old gypsy, the group of other boys moved in from behind and began encircling him. All of a sudden, Jadan fell down, diverting their attention. He was slumping and clutching the top of the cart. Then, his legs completely gave way. Jadan slowly eased down to the ground. Because Jadan was unable to help, Jerol felt lonely and afraid. The Badger winds rolled in from the north and began blowing across his arm, nudging the bottle in his hand up toward his lips.

The circle of boys was tightening, bringing the group within striking range. Obviously, friendship was not what they had on their minds! Their expressions were becoming more alarming with each step.

Jerol had seen enough to know that he was in danger. He quickly threw the bottle at the biggest brute of the bunch and pulled out his sword! The bottle bounced off the big boy's chest and tumbled to the ground, providing Jerol with just enough time to prepare for a fight.

One of the boys started pointing and laughing at Jerol; the rest of the group lifted their hands in unison. Immediately, eerie, grey, foul-smelling gas began bubbling up from the ground all around him. A weird, pale yellow mist began to lift from the mess, rising up and blending with the fog. Jerol began to sense an inexplicable force pulling him to the cart!

With no time to waste, he lifted his shield directly in front of his body and at the same time positioned his weapon over his head with the blade's tip pointing straight up. He thrust the sword skyward and shouted, "No temptation has seized you except what is common to Terrenea! I will provide you a way of escape" (Logos 46:10:13).

And with that, a spinning ball of white-hot light appeared and exploded directly above the sword's tip. The startled boys stopped their advance and gasped as the sparkling sphere began to throw off waves of intense light radiating out and away from the blade with increasing speed. As each wave intersected the yellowish fog, a blinding bright green light flashed out.

The gang sheltered their eyes and fell back, gripped in fear. The pulsating light slowly grew and moved down the blade, engulfing Jerol's upheld arm. The glow continued to move downward until culminating in a dazzling envelope of indescribable radiance around Jerol's entire body! Immediately, he felt the weight of the putrid mist disappear from his body! Light surrounded him with another flash, and then spiraled back up along the sword's glowing red blade. With a deafening crash, the beam vanished through an opening carved out through the fog.

During the commotion, Bacchus had disappeared into a hidden cave near the cart. The gang of boys that had looked so mean wanted no part of the strange light and had hurriedly scrambled behind Bacchus and into the safety of the cave.

Once Jerol was confident that all was clear, he walked over to the abandoned wagon and inspected some of its bottles. After a closer look, his suspicions were proved right. The cart was loaded down with mind-bending powders and such liquids as beers, liquors, and wines, just to mention a few! They were not only capable of dulling the mind, but ones' senses as well.

Several of the powders and potions even had the ability to make a person dependent on them for life. Once hooked, their victims would go through blackouts, shaking, and countless other unpleasant reactions if away from the potions for only a short period of time! Some poisons would even cause death if the user tried to stop taking them! And one of the poisons, corn cackle, was so vile that it could cause death after only one use!

Jerol recalled the Scroll's warning: "Wine is a mocker and beer a brawler; whoever is tricked by them is not Jerol. Do not get drunk on anything, which leads to poor decisions. Instead, be filled with the Logos" (Logos 20:20:1; 49:5:18). Even though Jerol felt tempted by the promise of relief, his discipline with the Logos had trained his conscience so well that his lack of peace about the Spirits had helped him to dodge potential disaster.

Turning his attention to his ailing brother, Jerol looked at the spot where Jadan had fallen. But he was not there! Jerol searched his surroundings and found his twin down the hill, passed out and lying on the side of the trail behind a minter bush. Jadan had fallen victim to one of Azrael's oldest tricks, promises of pleasure followed by a delivery of pain.

By this time, Sin had found his way back from his wild excursion in the hills and was curled up next to his sleeping partner. Jadan's snoring sounded like a two-man cross saw ripping through the trunk of an old hardwood tree! Jerol pushed and shoved on his brother, but he could not wake him. Sin tried to protect Jadan by standing between the brothers.

Quite annoyed, Jerol shooed Sin away! But the aggitated pig started grunting wildly, slinging his head from side to side and glaring at Jerol with his angry red eye. Jerol and Sin had never cared much for each other. If Jerol could have had his way, Jadan would have gotten rid of Sin many summers ago. But Jadan was just too attached to the pesky pig to let go. So, after much effort and with Prayer's help, Jerol finally chased Sin away. He then wrapped his arms around Jadan's chest from behind, dragged him to a nearby tree, and propped him up in a sitting position. And there they sat while Jerol tried to decide what to do next. The brothers were in a heap of trouble and needed a solid plan. Once again, Jerol did not know what to do or how. But of one thing he was certain. He would find a way out.

Chapter 21

Belle

"I find more bitter than death the woman who is a snare, whose heart is a trap and whose hands are chains. The man who pleases the King will escape her, but the simple she will ensnare."
Logos 21:7:26

Nighttime was fast approaching. To make matters worse, while Jerol and Jadan sat under the tree regrouping, it began to snow. And not just a little snow; the sky exploded with thousands of fat, wet flakes. In a short time, the ground was covered under a thin blanket of white!

Fortunately, over the last several days, Jerol had been studying the Scrolls and learning about the natural features of Terrenea. He felt confident that they were close to the village of Belle*. Considering his brother's weakened condition, the disappearing daylight and the unpredictable snow squall, Jerol decided that they needed to get to Belle as fast as they could.

Jerol looked at his brother. "He's not going to be able

to make it on his own, and I certainly can't leave him here," Jerol thought. "Not unprotected in this kind of weather." Jadan started to mumble. Jerol leaned in and strained to understand, but his words were all mixed up. Jerol was encouraged that Jadan seemed to be waking up. He was hopeful that his brother would be able to walk. So, he helped Jadan get back on his feet, but almost immediately he began to weave and stumble and then fell down again. The pitiful boy lay on his side in the middle of the cold, snow-laden path. The situation did not look good. Jerol knew he was not strong enough to carry his brother for long, for he and Jadan were about the same size.

Scratching his head, Jerol looked around, hoping an idea would come. Then his eyes focused through the falling snow on the abandoned cart. "That's it!" he shouted.

Jerol threw every box and bottle off the cart. He then wrapped one of Jadan's limp arms behind his neck and dragged him beside the empty wagon. Next, he gently draped his brother's body over the cart, and stuffed their belongings on each side.

If Jerol's hunch were right, they would arrive at Belle around dusk. By now, the snow was ankle deep. The descending curtain of white deadened all sound. The temperature was dropping and the way was getting more slippery with each passing moment. Jerol seized the wagon's handles in a white knuckled grip and strained ahead. "It will take more than a little snow shower to stop me," Jerol thought.

Luckily, Belle was at a much lower elevation, so the air should be a little warmer there. If Jerol's reckoning was right, this meant they would be leaving the snow behind.

Nighttime came earlier than he had expected. Jerol knew he was fatigued and becoming vulnerable to Azrael's tricks, but he tried his best to remain alert. His bothersome headache and having to cart Jadan down the mountainside had taken a lot out of him. Going downhill, Jerol had to lean back into the load to prevent it from careening off the mountain. Going up hill, he had to pull with all his might. He was physically spent and needed to find a safe place to rest his weary bones.

With his head straining forward and teeth clenched, Jerol forced one foot in front of the other until he was able to see the warm, yellow lights of Belle. "Look, brother. There it is! We're almost there!" Jerol shouted. With a renewed spirit he trudged forward with aching shoulders and burning legs until passing the town's welcome sign. Exhausted, he dropped the cart handles and fell to his hands and knees. Jerol had somehow managed to get them inside the city limits.

Belle was a special community. The village lay on the eastern side of Euphoria. This unique city is one of only two locations in Terrenea where only women live. The other place is Éclat*, a beautiful valley nestled between the gorgeous foothills of the Seraphic* mountains to the west and the mountains of Maiden to the east. Men from all across Bravura travel to these enchanted places to find wives.

Well, leaving the cart behind, Jerol and Jadan entered the town and began searching for a friendly face. Jadan was walking again, but still showing signs of the Spirit's influence. A young woman who was on her way to one of the local shops caught their eye. Jerol waved her down and asked if she knew of a safe place where he and Jadan could spend the night.

She hesitated, then, with a smile and a wink, suggested, "Why don't you try the Fantasy Inn, just two blocks down?"

Too tired to notice her flirtation, Jerol thanked her and led Jadan to the inn's front porch. Jadan was giddy, loud, and drawing unwanted attention. Jerol knew that they needed to find a room quickly before Jadan could get them in trouble. Once inside the inn, another friendly girl greeted them.

"Kind lady, do you have a room for my brother and me to spend the night?" Jerol queried.

In the meantime, Jadan had worked his way to another part of the lobby and was creating a commotion with three lovely young ladies, two of whom were petting Sin and laughing hysterically. Jadan was leaning on one of them with his arm around her shoulders. Their laughter drew Jerol's eyes toward them.

All at once, a sensation that Jerol had never felt before staggered him. The third girl, who was quietly standing and listening to Jadan and the other two girls, captured Jerol's full attention. She was staring at him, and, when their eyes met, she quickly looked away.

As she turned her head, her eyes seemed to possess some kind of magnetic force that pulled Jerol to her! In fact, every girl in Belle had this same strange, magical power. This power, if honored and respected as the Logos taught, could more than double a man's strength. However, abusing it had led some of the King's most noble champions to ruin!

Curious, Jerol walked over to meet her. "Hello. My name is Jerol. What's yours?"

She smiled sweetly and replied, "Grace*."

Their introduction was cut short by Jadan's rude interruption. "Hey, Jerol! My new friends, Jezebel* and Delilah* are going to a wedding tonight! Two of their girlfriends are getting married. And afterwards they have invited us to the wedding celebration! They said there would be lots of food, wine, and dancing. Sounds like a good time! What do you say, Brother?"

"Pardon me Grace. I need to talk with my brother for just a moment." Jerol motioned for Jarad over so he could share his thoughts without being rude to the girls. "Better be careful Jarad!" Jerol whispered. "I don't have a good feeling about this. We need to stay focused on getting to Sentinel. Those girls don't look like the kind of girls that the King would approve of." He said glancing at Delilah and Jezebel. "Just look at the way they are dressed. I think you had better think again before going with them."

"Oh, come on, Jerol. There you go again." Jadan shouted. "Loosen up, would ya! Those old scrolls are nothing more than a bunch of trumped up fairy tales! When are you going to start living in the real world?"

Little did the twins know that Belle would turn out to be one of the most dangerous places they would pass through on their way to Sentinel. Azrael had scores of followers there. Most of the girls living in Belle practiced his religion of pleasure and were usually up to no good.

Even though Jerol knew in his heart that there was danger, deep inside he felt his curiosity beginning to stir. Before he had time to respond, a large man burst across the room and stormed straight over to Grace. "I'll take you missy!" he bellowed. "Let's go! You're coming with me!" Grace struggled to pull away.

Jerol ran to the man and firmly exclaimed, "Hey, what do you think you're doing? Let her go!"

Firmly holding onto Grace, the big brute cut his

beady eyes toward Jerol. The burly intruder was part of a group of giants known as the Hellions*. He was twice Jerol's size and obviously not in a friendly mood. "And who are *you*, little boy?" he growled.

"My name is Jerol. I serve Deus, the King of Light and am from the city of Gelandesprung. My brother and I are on our way to Sentinel."

"Oh, really?" the man sneered. "Well, I don't know who you think you are, squirt, but I came here to get me a girl, and this one will do just fine for me. So, if you don't want more trouble than you can handle, you'd better step aside!"

Seeing that Grace's welfare was at stake, Jerol grabbed the giant's arm in both hands and shoved, jarring Grace loose from his grip. Then Jerol jumped back, drew out his sword and stepped between her and the startled giant.

The angry intruder muttered something under his breath, reached down and unsheathed a blade that was at least two times bigger than the boy's! The two stood sizing each other up. The Hellion made the first move, lunging down with the point of his sword straight at Jerol's face! Jerol confidently stepped aside bringing the solid edge of his blade across and down, deflecting the blow.

In one down-and-then-up-again motion, Jerol blocked and rapidly brought the edge of his blade up at the giant's bulging neck. The agile oaf moved aside as the thin metal of Jerol's sword sliced through the air within a thumb's width past his nose! The warriors stood again, facing each another in locked gaze.

The clever Hellion faked a strike to Jerol's upper left arm. The brave lad instinctively moved his shield to block. The deceiver quickly changed course, moving his blade with a crushing side blow denting Jerol's breastplate. Jerol spun off balance, stumbled over some chairs and crashed against a wall of stone! Pain traveled through his chest and upper arm. He could not draw a breath! The stunned boy dropped his sword and slumped to the floor.

The anxious brute quickly took advantage and moved in to finish off the helpless boy! Jerol struggled to get back on his feet, but could not! The giant was on top of him with his sword held high above and behind his head!

Quickly glancing from side to side, Jerol spotted his sword lying on the floor within arm's reach. While grabbing at his sword, he kicked forward making contact with one of the giant's thick shins. The momentum of the Hellion's advance kept him from adjusting himself. The great oaf began to rotate about Jerol's foot with his upper body in rapid descent. The contest ended in a loud crash and a billowing cloud of dust. When the air cleared, the giant was lying on top of Jerol amid broken glass and a heap of overturned chairs and tables. Each lay motionless.

By this time a crowd of curious folks had gathered to watch the fight. People were standing around waiting to see if the boy was all right. Jadan and the girls rushed over to where they lay. "Jerol! Jerol!" Jadan yelled. There was still no movement. Jadan and Grace labored frantically to pull the giant's limp body off Jerol, then knelt down to check for breathing. Jerol let out a quick blurt of air. "He's alive!" Grace shouted. The room erupted with applause and cheers!

Jerol slowly sat up and began inspecting the damage. He was banged up, but luckily, nothing serious. By some miracle Jerol's sword had stood straight up just before the Hellion fell on top of him. Regretfully, the giant had been mortally wounded.

Jerol was saddened that the stranger was dead. However, he had fulfilled his duty as spelled out in the Logos: "He will defend the afflicted among the people and save the children of the needy; he will crush the oppressor. Honor girls by defending them when they are in physical danger" (Logos 19:10:14; 19:35:10; 19:55:22; 19:82:3; 60:3:7) The King's will had been done and Grace was safe.

Grace knelt down, politely hugging her reluctant hero. "Thank you, kind sir," she whispered. "I will never forget this day and the brave warrior who fought for my honor. I will be forever in your debt."

Jerol blushed from ear to ear. "Dear lady, I will forever be at your service."

Standing nearby and yawning with disinterest, Jezebel had seen enough. "Boys," she snapped, "if we're going to make it to the wedding, we'd better get going! Jadan, are you coming with me or not?"

It was obvious that her despicable spell had taken full affect. Like a dog on a leash, Jadan moved away from Jerol and followed Jezebel through a red door at the back of the lobby. The other girl, Delilah, fixed her attention on Jerol.

"Are you coming with me, brave warrior?" she purred,

moving to him. "You must be tired from your travels and sore from your fight. Come, let me take care of you." She began walking toward him.

Jerol could feel the pull of Delilah's tempting stare! Grace stood, wide-eyed, watching in silence, first looking at her one-time friend and then at Jerol. How could he defend against such an evil spell?

Once again Jerol searched his memory for guidance. He recalled what the Logos taught: "Do not desire in your heart after the beauty of the evil woman or let her trap you with her eyes. She preys upon your life. Can a man scoop fire into his lap without his clothes being burned? Can a man walk on hot coals without his feet being scorched? Therefore, leave your cloak in her hand and run out of the house" (Logos 20:6:25-28; 1:39:12).

At once, Jerol sprang to his feet! "I'm sorry, Grace. Forgive me, but I must go! Do not forget me!" he shouted as he ran from the inn as fast as his wobbly legs could take him! He ran and ran and ran until he reached the fringe of the village lights.

Luckily a full moon lit the sky that night. Jerol stopped and doubled over, gasping for air. He was dead tired. After facing Bacchus, transporting his brother down the mountain, and tussling with the Hellion, he was struggling to stay awake. But, then a flash of light up ahead shocked him to his senses. There was a glimmer of something moving back inside the shadows of the trees just up ahead! "What could it be this time?" He wondered. Glimmers of light flashed out every time the breeze blew. Whatever it was; it seemed to be stationary.

Jerol cautiously walked over for a better look. It appeared as if something was hanging from a tree limb. The thing was barely visible and dangling far back in the darkness near the trunk of a tree. Jerol walked over, warily reached in and then pulled the object out level with his eyes.

He could not believe what he saw! The object was not one, but two golden keys! Could he be dreaming? On one he could see the outline of the word SERVICE sparkling in the moonlight! On the other was engraved the word INTEGRITY! Jerol was beginning to see a pattern.

Just like the key before, he had not found it, but the key somehow had found him! After displaying submission to the Logos during a time of crisis, soon afterwards a key would miraculously appear!

Because of his obedience to the Logos in defending Grace, he had displayed the highest level of concern for the protection of his fellow Terreneans. For this he had earned the key of Service. For turning away from the different temptations of Coveton and Euphoria he had been given the key of Integrity.

He concluded that the common thread was plainly obedience. So, he recommitted to following the teaching of the Logos. Now, he understood that obeying its guidance was his only hope for success.

Thinking that a return to the village would be too risky, Jerol found a comfortable spot in the pine grove to spend the rest of the night. He added the new keys to the key of Courage already hanging on the ring of the sword's handle. He scooped up a generous pile of pine needles into a boy-sized bed and burrowed deeply underneath his cozy cloak.

He lay there thinking about Grace and how someday he would return to find her. As he looked with profound satisfaction at the keys that he had worked so hard to find, exhaustion quickly overtook him, and he collapsed into a deep and rewarding sleep.

He had traveled more than halfway to Sentinel! Nothing would stop him now.

Chapter 22

Gevah

"In his pride the wicked does not seek him; in all his thoughts there is no room for the King." Logos 19:10:4

Three summers had passed since Jerol left Belle and the Mountain of Pleasure. Life on the road was not getting easier. In fact, some days he questioned whether he would even go on. But, somehow, Jerol always found enough determination to keep moving. So, he continued to labor ahead until at last he could see the jungle's uneven outline on the distant horizon. Gevah, the Jungle of Pride, had prevented more boys from reaching Sentinel than all the other challenges combined. Jerol was not looking forward to the battles that were to come. But, if he wanted to receive the Mark, he would somehow have to conquer the dangers that awaited him.

Jerol often questioned whether he had made the right decision in leaving Belle without Jadan. But just as he had done many times since escaping, he remembered that there had been no other choice. He had not abandoned his brother. Instead, Jadan had decided to stay.

Even so, Jerol thought often about his brother's welfare. "I hope he's okay. I wish that there were some way that I could help him," he thought. "Oh, well. I can't live his life for him. We all have to find our own way. I can't let my concern for Jadan defeat me, too." Jerol studied for a while. "I know what I can do. I will send out Prayer on his behalf. Prayer is so much stronger than I am and can do so much more to help him." So, Jerol penned a note and launched Prayer back to Belle in search of Jadan. Once Jerol was satisfied that he had done all that he could do for his brother, he continued his trek to Gevah. After only three days travel, Prayer returned. He had delivered Jerol's note and resumed his watch, circling above. Jerol had hoped that Jadan would have sent a note back with Prayer, but Prayer had returned empty-handed.

It took another half of a day before Jerol stood at the jungle's outer edge. As he often did, he sent Prayer out and over the jungle to scout the way. He waited patiently until his trusted comrade had circled back and signaled that he could safely enter. Following Prayer's lead, Jerol pulled his sword, hacked a gap through a web of tangled vines and made his way into the shadows.

The Jungle was wet and musty. Tall trees supported an over-arching canopy full of life high above the jungle floor. Strings of water droplets fell like strands of clear beads from the tops of the trees. Thick undergrowth shrouded the trail from view. But nothing was going to stop this determined soul. As usual, Jerol remained resolute and persisted pushing farther into the unknown.

One particular morning, Jerol began his day as he had many times before. First, he searched the Scrolls for direction. This discipline had proved its worth like a candle in the dark, helping him often to avoid unseen dangers. He then called Prayer and launched him off with more notes for Jadan and the King. Then, after completing his morning disciplines, Jerol set out down the trail.

About midmorning the wind began to pick up speed and the jungle steadily grew darker. Jerol could hear distant thunder echoing from somewhere above the forest's lofty ceiling. Gevah was notorious for sudden downpours and violent storms. Because of the dense vegetation, you could never tell exactly how far away the storm might be. In fact, the overgrowth was so crowded that, since entering the jungle, Jerol had been able to see the sky only rarely.

The Jungle of Pride was an unpredictable place. Sometimes the sky would rain so hard that, in the low-lying areas, flash floods would rise in a matter of moments, wiping out everything in their paths. At other times, though, the fickle storm would rumble past without releasing a single drop.

We had taught Jadan and Jerol that staying alert was a traveler's best bet. Asking "What if . . ." questions and then having a good plan to deal with the consequences usually helped to lessen painful surprises.

So, Jerol asked himself. "What if a flash flood comes at me? What should I do?" He figured that he was probably in a low-lying part of the jungle because he could see a small stream about ten steps away. So, he determined to not go any father until he had located nearby trees that he could climb should the waters begin to rise.

Periodically, thunder would boom and echo far overhead. Always surrounded by uncertainty, Jerol did not flinch. He moved forward while keeping an eye out for signs of danger. He was determined that no solitary storm would ever push him back. Besides, he had faced many storms before. He was not afraid. As always, he would trust the Logos to see him through.

Chapter 23

Puffers

"Don't be pleasers of yourselves, but in humility consider others better than yourselves."
Logos 50:2:3

Fortunately, this day the storm had decided to pass by without making a scene. Jerol had been traveling nonstop since morning, and the time was about halfway between midday and dusk. As he pushed on to the heart of Pride, noise began to build high up in the top of a nearby tree. Normally, the animals of the jungle were much quieter during daylight. So, Jerol knew that something was not right. The curious lad stopped to see what was causing the commotion. The racket was coming from a rare break in the foliage where the sun was peaking through. He shaded his eyes and looked up, but the only thing he could see was a flock of agitated birds chattering and flapping their wings.

While he was watching the canopy above, the jungle chatter exploded in a clash of animal screams! Out of the nearby bushes popped four elfin creatures! Jerol stood perfectly still and stared at them as they stared back. They were standing only about six steps away! The tops of their heads were level with Jerol's knees! Their heads were round, bald, and shiny and as wide as their bodies. They had bushy eyebrows, big green eyes, plump red noses, and wide mouths full of large flat teeth. They had almost no neck to speak of and bodies that were squatty with small flabby arms hanging down to their waists. Their hands looked much wider than their arms. Their clothes were densely dotted from head to toe with countless bits of shiny metal. Jerol felt sure they were Puffers, a primitive race of elves known to inhabit the jungle.

The Puffers* were made up of three distinctive clans. Of their close-knit communities, the most dominant group was known as the Selfs. They were bald, short, and round and these intruders standing before Jerol definitely fit that description.

Selfs were known for having unpredictable personalities and for being extremely independent. Depending on their mood, they could be the closest friends or the fiercest enemies of Terrenea! So, not knowing if these four were dangerous or not, Jerol took no chances. He eased into a defensive stance and slowly moved his hand toward the handle of his sword. Seeing that the boy was reaching for his weapon, all four of the strangers dropped to their knees. One of them lowered his head while slowly spreading his arms straight out from his sides. He then presented his empty palms—the sign of peace. Once the sign of peace was offered, the elf kneeling to his right began to speak. As the Puffer opened his big mouth, Jerol was surrounded by a curious sense of warmth.

"Please, don't hurt. Mean no harm. Us are Selfs and this is homeland. For yesterdays have been looking at you. Told leader that you look like friend. So, he send back to invite you to big eat time to say welcome. Us say same to all friends. Leader be sad if you say no".

Jerol felt beaten up from wrestling with the jungle. Spending a little time with these guys looked like a refreshing change. "Besides," he thought, "they want to show me some hospitality. How can I say no to that?" Jerol trusted that they were really telling the truth.

Showing the sign of peace, Jerol responded, "I'd be honored to be your guest. I have heard of your people and would like to learn more about you and your customs."

The kneeling Selfs jumped up, and clapped their hands, obviously pleased with Jerol's answer. So, after a brief conversation, they led Jerol off the narrow path and onto a concealed course leading south and deeper through the jungle.

Narcissa*, the overcrowded village of the Selfs was nestled in the heart of the jungle. Wide streets of rounded stones wove in between shelters of different sizes. These hut-like dwellings were made from a mixture of dried mud and leaves. The streets were busy and crowded with Puffers bumping against one another and moving in every direction. They escorted Jerol to a hut prepared specially for honored guests where he remained until sundown.

Several villagers attended to Jerol as he waited patiently to make his entrance at the community table. Again, he noticed a curious sensation of great warmth and comfort whenever his hosts would speak to him. The feeling was odd but pleasurable.

Immediately after sunset, he was escorted to the village ceremonial hut where he was greeted by Heinous, the village leader. Heinous was a friendly, kind, charming fellow and appeared overjoyed that Jerol had accepted his invitation. The flabbergasted boy leaned down so his new friends could lavish him with flowers and gifts. After much lively conversation, the jolly hosts stayed true to their word and treated Jerol to the best meal he had eaten since leaving Gelandesprung! The food was spread out before him like a king. He stuffed his face with pheasant, pork, chicken, beef, and fish, all grilled over a sweet smoky fire stoked with brazzleberry wood. There were potatoes, beans, corn, campfire bread and a delicious dessert made from heaping helpings of wild blueberries and strawberries and, to top it off, they presented Jerol with a rare treat of lemon leaf tea sweetened with a dash of honeysuckle nectar.

After finishing the feast, the satisfied boy and his hosts lumbered down next to the cozy fire where Heinous promised to restock Jerol's supplies, and even told him that they had information that would help him find the final key! Impressed by their great generosity, Jerol decided to spend several more days. They were constantly bragging on everything he did and said. Day after day they showered him with nothing but praise. Jerol was growing fond of his new friends and was in no hurry to leave.

Before too long, however, he began to notice something that he thought was odd. The impish creatures were changing appearance and growing taller. Many Puffers had grown to be twice his height in just a few days' time!

Their small stocky shapes had gradually transformed into tall, lean, muscular bodies. Their tiny limbs had changed into powerful arms and legs, and they had grown hair on their heads and long grey beards that, on some, reached clear down to their knees! Jerol obviously found the changes to be strange, but he reasoned that they were of a different race and must develop differently from his people. Terrenea was a huge place. There was much that he had not yet seen or done. Who was he to judge?

Well, the more appreciation Jerol gave them, the faster they grew. Their response to Jerol's attention was like pouring water on a starving weed. One day Jerol witnessed a couple of Selfs pull down a small tree using only their bare hands!

Puzzled and uncomfortable, Jerol watched as the Puffer's carefree behavior took a nasty turn; they went from praising him to trying to control him. And they were becoming aggressive. The bigger guys had even started pushing him around. Jerol was disturbed by the new way they were beginning to treat him and decided to leave Narcissa at the next opportune time.

So one night Jerol made plans to leave early the next morning before the Selfs had gotten out of bed. He retired at his usual time, not wanting to raise their suspicions, and, late that night, he secretly packed.

Later in the night, Jerol was abruptly awakened by the sound of agitated voices. He quickly sat up and cleared the sleep from his eyes. There were Selfish giants on every side of him, and he could see in their faces that, this time, they had not come for a friendly visit! What Jerol failed to know was that a Puffer's purpose in life is to find an unsuspecting soul and slowly poison him with larkspur. Larkspur is a potent toxin of flattery expelled in hot air. Following each release of larkspur, the victim becomes more attached to the Puffer, and the Puffer grows into a more mature form of creature known as a Bigot. Bigots* are giants that enslave their captives then eventually trade them for materials and goods. Sometimes the giants choose victims for a hideous form of entertainment called the Deathmatch. If you are unable to break free from their maniacal clutches, doom will finally be your fate. For Jerol, he had waited too long to make his getaway. He did not have time to grab anything. In an instant, they had him crisscrossed and bound with sturdy ropes!

The Bigots seemed to be in a hurry and wasted no time shoving him through the door of his hut to the outside where two more giants were waiting. They nabbed him, restraining him on each side. By all appearances, the rest of the village had assembled just outside his hut and were waiting for him to be led out and into their midst. Jerol noticed that another giant, just up ahead and to his left, had the boy's belongings strapped on his back.

The crowd began shuffling apart and clearing a path for Heinous. The Bigot leader had grown even taller than the rest and was an imposing character. He was loud and aggressive. The crowd grew silent as he stepped up, leaned over, and pushed his nose within about two hands from the tip of Jerol's nose and snarled.

"You be stupid boy. You too important to you. When you too important to you, then we grow strong. When we grow strong, we rule. Now you do as we want. You be chosen for game. It is our way." The air coming from Heninous' mouth felt as hot as the air around a fire.

Heinous then turned to the Bigot with Jerol's backpack and barked the order—"Hurry, they be waiting." With that about a dozen giants moved into a circle around Jerol. The giant carrying the backpack took a position in the front. They then followed Heinous and the crowd to the edge of the village clearing.

Heinous raised his arms and exclaimed, "We serve Azrael! Azrael alone! Be off!"

As the band of wicked soldiers marched into the shade of the jungle, the crowd erupted in chants of "Azrael!, Azrael!"

For the next several days, the cruel scalawags led Jerol through the hot humid jungle like an animal on a leash, stopping only to rest and eat. Jerol wondered where they were taking him. "The game? What was Henious talking about?" he thought to himself.

"What are they going to do with me?" he wanted to know. Jerol was sorry that he had fallen for their tricks and lies. Looking back, he could see how he had been poisoned. At the time, he had been weakened by the struggle of the journey. And, to his weary heart their warm words were like a soothing balm. He vowed, "Next time I will be ready. I will spend more time with Prayer. I will stay more alert."

"Move, dog!" growled the lead giant, yanking on the

rough rope that was tied to Jerol's sore neck.

Jerol felt anger swelling deep inside because of his captors' arrogance and cruelty. But, he would not fight back now. He would be patient and wait for the right opportunity to make his escape.

Chapter 24

Gascon

"Stay on the alert. Your enemy prowls around like a roaring beast, looking for someone to eat." Logos 60:5:8

Finally, the boy and his captors arrived before a colossal structure. Jerol drew back his head and looked straight up its side. He guessed the wall was at least ten times his height. The walls were made of massive square sandstones, tightly stacked beside and on top of one another. He could hear many loud voices, as though a crowd were gathered inside. The great structure reminded Jerol of the historic coliseum of Perfidy.

Perfidy* was one of the oldest settlements in Terrenea. The city was an unruly place where violent battles were held before wild spectators. If the place were anything like Perfidy, Jerol did not want to be there.

The giants paused just outside a large arched doorway. High up on top of the wall another Bigot signaled to Jerol's party. The lumbering giants then steered Jerol into the opening and through the sandstone wall. Once on the other side, Jerol looked up across the circular stands where many giants stood ranting and raving. He could barely hear the beat of a drum above the noise of the crowd. The drum's steady cadence had an unsettling tone of dreadful expectancy.

The brutal guards jerked Jerol from the shadows and into the crowd's view, cheers exploded from everywhere with a deafening roar! They dragged him to the center of the arena and wrestled him down onto a bloodstained, rickety, wooden chair scarred with many gaping scratches. The chair was sitting back to back with another chair in the middle of a circle that was roughly ten steps wide and cut in the dirt. Before Jerol was seated, he caught a glimpse of another boy sitting in the other chair, faced in the opposite direction. He was then quickly bound with ropes, anchoring him to his chair. As the guards strutted to leave the stadium, Jerol leaned back and spoke a quick and nervous word of encouragement to the other boy. "Don't worry; I know we will figure a way out of this."

To his astonishment, the voice he heard from the other chair was the voice of Jadan! "Jerol, is that you?" Jadan shouted. "Oh, Brother, isn't it amazing? Can you believe it? The Selfs have honored us with the best seats in the whole place!"

Jadan's words made no sense. "Surely he is ill," Jerol thought. Jadan seemed unafraid.

Jerol sensed that the crowd was quickly growing impatient, for their jeers and boos grew louder with each beat of the drum. They seemed to be waiting for something to happen. At once a sharp trumpet blast sounded and the coliseum grew silent. A distant voice began echoing something into the stands. As the crowd's attention focused on the speaker, Jerol took the opportunity to scan the curving walls encircling the theater's base. He noticed that his belongings had been thrown on the ground next to his chair. He quickly spotted his sword and armor, and located Jadan's belongings arranged in a similar fashion.

Jadan had obviously been brainwashed by the giants into thinking he was still their guest of honor. Somehow they had convinced him that the chairs in which he and Jerol sat were the best seats in the house. So Jadan just sat there, naively waiting for the games to start. He thought that he was about to witness some kind of sporting event, unaware that he and Jerol were the main attraction.

The sun was shining on Jerol's half of the arena floor while Jadan's side lay hidden in the shade of the great structure's wall. Jerol tugged on the ropes holding him to the chair. They felt loose! Bigots may be capable at pushing boys around, but they are lousy at tying knots. Jerol began moving his arms up and down. To his surprise, the ropes began to slip down the back of his chair. In just a few jerks he had worked his way free. Not wasting a moment, he quickly knelt down, threw on his helmet, and scooped up his weapon and shield.

Just as Jerol touched his sword, the announcer finished his speech, and another loud trumpet blast rang out. Sounds of rattling chains and ferocious roars coming from behind an enormous door began to fill the hushed arena. The crowd leapt to its feet, cheering and stomping in unison at the arrival of some sort of wild beast.

Jerol glued his eyes on the huge wooden door as it slowly began to creak upward. He could see frenzied movement followed by a billow of dust blowing out from underneath the door's bottom edge. He focused and readied himself, watching intensely as the door continued to climb.

Once it was halfway open, a clawing, screaming animal broke free, rattling the great door, and charged for the center of the ring. The awesome creature was at least ten steps long, and each of its feet was easily the size of Jerol's head. It was lean and taut with fangs as long as a hand and claws churning up hard arena dirt in a cloud of choking dust. The arena began to fill with chants of "Gascon*…Gascon…Gascon!" The Logos taught of a legendary behemoth that roamed Gevah day and night constantly looking to maim and destroy. Some of its most desired victims were young, innocent boys on their way to Sentinel. Ruthless with a heart of stone, it was infamous for having a single lust—Terrenean blood!

Jerol had already faced difficult trials on his quest, but this time he would be challenged beyond the limits of his strength and character.

He knew that he was in a desperate situation, because he had not kept up his guard. The Logos' warned that "pride goes before destruction, a selfish spirit before a fall"(Logos 20:16:18). Azrael had used the Puffers laid-back manner to lull Jerol and Jadan into a false sense of confidence which had clouded the brother's minds so that they did not even see the dangerous traps the evil ruler had waiting for them.

Jerol decided that if he survived the test, he would not make the same mistake again. He would admit his error and recommit fully to the quest. So, even in the midst of his fear, he renewed his faith in the wisdom of the Logos and set his face like flint at the advancing terror.

He locked eyes with the heaving monster as it closed in fast. Gascon halted his advance in a spray of dirt clods that riddled Jerol's shield in rapid succession! The great brute began pacing just a few steps away. He moved back and forth, hissing and drooling, looking for an opening. Jerol felt the beast's tremendous power jarring the ground with each pounding step. Impatiently circling his prey, Gascon licked his huge jowls as he appeared to be sizing up Jadan and Jerol for his midday meal.

Jadan still did not grasp the danger he was in and

remained spellbound, patiently sitting in his seat. "Unbelievable!" Jadan shouted. "I can almost reach out and touch this magnificent creature!"

Gascon immediately focused on the jabbering boy. In an instant, the great demon cat charged at Jadan and with one mighty swat sent him and his chair flying, flipping through the air, halfway across the stadium floor! Jadan landed beside his broken overturned chair in a crumpled heap. The crowd jumped to its feet, wild with applause and cheers.

In one continuous motion, Gascon reversed direction, took a couple of explosive steps, and vaulted toward Jerol. Jerol sidestepped the charging threat, using his shield to push against it as it passed by. The great cat weighed at least twenty times more than Jerol, causing the boy to be deflected by the force of the collision and stumbling to catch his balance.

Gascon landed on all fours, shook his big head, and bellowed a thunderous roar that shook the entire arena. The angry cat exposed a large trap of fangs, preparing to rip at Jerol! The crowd hushed as their beloved champion spun in a cloud of dust to face Jerol again. The two opponents began walking in a circle facing one another, first in one direction, then in the other.

Someone in the crowd threw a pebble that struck Jerol on his left shoulder. He instinctively moved his head and, for an instant, took his eyes off the beast. In the brief moment it took for him to look back, the cunning monster pounced like a hungry cat at a mouse! The great animal's powerful legs pounded furiously as he sprang straight for Jerol's throat. The force of the Gascon's sudden movement shook the ground.

Jerol had just enough room to slide his shield between them and was knocked backwards by what, he later told me, felt like the weight of a hundred sacks of corn. Jerol fell on his back with a crunching thud. Gascon stood with one paw pressing down, pinning Jerol between his shield and the arena floor. The unrelenting cat began to rake his other paw underneath to finish him off.

Jerol was tightly locked in an awkward position. His right arm was the only part of his body not pinned down. The heavy weight of the great beast made it difficult for Jerol to breathe. Fortunately, the collision and fall had not dislodged the sword from Jerol's grip. Jerol quickly tucked the sword back underneath the shield.

As Gascon groped and ripped under the shield, the tenderest part of his enormous paw met with the edge of Jerol's sword. The big cat quickly retreated and let out ear-piercing screams of fury! The outburst gave Jerol just enough time to scramble back onto his feet.

Meanwhile, at the other end of the arena, Jadan started waking up. He raised up on his hands and knees, and shook his head. Gascon saw another opportunity and closed ground. The beast released his anger and frustration with another numbing blow to the helpless boy! This time Jadan tumbled across the ground like a giant rag doll before stopping in a twisted heap.

Showing unusual patience, the predator slowly crept toward the helpless lad. Jerol knew that his brother was in serious trouble. Hoping that Gascon was distracted, Jerol ran full speed at its back, moving his blade in a figure eight pattern. But, Gascon spotted Jerol out of the corner of his eye and reeled sideways just in time to escape the silver blur of the sword. Now, for the first time, the great beast appeared to be concerned and on the defense. Gascon sensed that Jerol was not afraid as

other boys had been; such courage had caught the brute off guard.

With one paw injured and a determined boy in hot pursuit, Gascon decided to retreat. Somehow, the startled cat managed to dodge two more of Jerol's attacks before moving back to the opened door from which it had entered. Jerol sensed the monster's growing fear and continued pressing his assault until Gascon's stubby tail had passed back under the great arch of stone.

Jerol spotted a heavy rope anchored to a wooden stake in the ground and just to the right of the door. The rope was tied to the top of the door and holding it up. Moving swiftly, he cut the rope with his blade and dropped the heavy panel into the dirt with a great thud. Wasting no time, Jerol quickly spun back for his brother as the cowardly cat stood trembling, trapped on the outside of the arena's wall.

As Jerol ran to Jadan, he noticed an eerie, almost deafening, silence. A muffled rumble began moving through the crowd. He looked up to see what was happening. The great coliseum was no longer filled with seething giants, but instead with little Puffers! Somehow their size had been affected by Gascon's failure. They were not pleased with being small again. You might say they were mad, and Jerol knew that even though they were small in size, because there was so many of them there would be no margin for error. He quickly scanned the stadium for a way out, but to his dismay there were no clear exits to be found! They were trapped!

Scores of angry Selfs began jumping over the side barriers from every direction and onto the arena floor. “There is just no way to defeat so many!” Jerol thought.

Moving quickly he lifted the handle of his sword and unscrewed its end. Once opened, the handle revealed a small tubular compartment. Holding the sword in his left hand, Jerol quickly emptied its contents, raised it to his mouth, and began to blow with all his might!

It was a shiny silver stick, about one hand long and wide as a thumb. It had a hole in its top and a smaller hole in one end. The special whistle emitted a shrill note that caused earsplitting pain to the advancing Selfs. Just as Jerol had hoped, the piercing tone seemed to be slowing them down. He knew, though, that before long their great numbers would overwhelm him.

Just as they reached out to nab him, Prayer swooped down, answering Jerol’s call for help. Catching him by a breastplate strap the awesome bird jerked Jerol up and out of harm’s way.

One of the more determined dwarfs had somehow grabbed onto one of Jerol’s ankles and was ranting and jerking down with his hands while dangling in midair! Jerol tried to kick him off, but the rascal refused to let go. After clearing the top ledge of the stadium’s upper deck, Prayer dove straight down at a couple of trees near the arena's outer court and, with great ease, adjusted his flight to avoid a head-on collision. The pesky imp raked hard across the outer branches of the tree and was knocked free. The screaming Puffer tumbled down, snapping through four weak branches before coming to rest in an area of closely grouped limbs. Jerol could hear him cursing as they flew away.

Prayer carried Jerol through the night. The moon was full, bright, and beautiful. Tired and weary from battle, the boy dozed in and out as moonlight flashed across his face through passing clouds. Sometime shortly after daybreak, Prayer landed in a clearing on top of The Eye*, a tall rocky mesa overlooking and surrounded by more jungle. Once on the ground, Jerol immediately sent Prayer back to rescue Jadan and find the rest of his belongings. Normal birds would have been weakened by the previous night's work. But Prayer was a Royal falcon. The awesome bird did not hesitate and sprang up like a giant stone flung from a mighty sling, whipping the air, displacing dust and leaves in all directions. Jerol sheltered his face as best he could and stepped behind a sturdy tree until Prayer was well above the jungle.

From his elevated vantage point, Jerol was excited to see that the Wall of Devoir surrounding Sentinel was just over the eastern horizon. With his bearings set, he would soon be standing near the city limits of Sentinel. Jerol could hardly believe it! However, concerned for his brother's welfare, he decided to patiently wait for Prayer's return before moving on to the city.

Shortly after the midday meal, Jerol was startled by his backpack falling from the sky and landing just a

few steps from where he was seated. "My pack!" Jerol shouted as he jumped up to greet his returning friend. Prayer descended and landed beside him. "Where is my brother?" Jerol implored. Prayer hung his head and began scratching in the dirt. Jerol slumped to the ground and began to weep. He was afraid Jadan had not survived. Prayer leaned down and gently nudged him with the top of his downy soft head. Jerol looked up to see what he wanted. Clasped in the bird's powerful beak was a beautiful golden tube. Jerol gently removed the tiny cylinder from his partner's mouth, opened it, and pulled out a rolled-up note. He unfurled the paper and through tear-filled eyes began to read.

Jerol,

*You have conquered the captivity of Pride! Your journey, I know, has been long and sometimes hard. At times it has even been frightening. But you have persevered in your obedience to me. You have but one key left to find. Press on. You must not give up. When you arrive at the hallowed Wall of Devoir**, be extremely cautious about which door you choose to enter. Do not be deceived. Azrael has placed several traps, disguised as gates, as part of the wall. However, there is only one true door. Remember, a willing spirit is the mortar that holds the great wall* *in place. If your heart is lazy, beware, for the wall may fall and crush you. To enter my court, you must find the one true gate. Before entering, examine your heart to see if you are worthy to stand in the presence of the Blades who have come before. Know this: only those who enter through the right door and are worthy will receive my full blessing. I eagerly await your arrival.*

King Deus

CHAPTER 25

The Green River

"In all these things, we are more than conquerors through Paladin, who loves us." LOGOS 45:8:37

Still grieving from his fear that Jadan might be dead, Jerol reluctantly charted what he hoped would be the last part of his journey. Once again he sent Prayer out to scout ahead. During the past few moons, Jerol had discovered that Prayer's perspective was far better than his own, for Prayer could see the "big picture" from above; Jerol's sight was limited by his close surroundings. In a little while, Prayer circled back and signaled that the way was clear.

The forest in this part of Gevah seemed to be even more challenging than the other areas he had traversed. Travel was slow. At one point, Jerol began to notice strange vibrations underneath his feet. The farther he walked, the greater they became. In time, he began to hear a steady, muffled rumble that seemed to match the rhythm of the vibration. Sticks and leaves were moving on the ground in sync with the sound.

"Whatever it is, it's gonna be huge!" Jerol thought with intense curiosity.

Before long, the sound was as loud as the stampede of a herd of Bovines. Puzzled, Jerol forged ahead, until a line of thick bushes stopped him. He pulled his sword and cut out a section of tall reeds that blocked his view. When he stepped through to the other side, the view opened wide along the jungle's back edge. Raging before him, and only a stone's throw away, was an enormous river of churning green water!

He looked across the channel to the riverbank on the other side, which seemed to be a hundred or so steps away. Just beyond he could see a stand of tall timber followed by a cliff of varying heights. And resting along the cliff's rising ridge stood a dark stone wall. The river formed a moat surrounding the circle of timber and wall as far as he could see. Jerol's heart began to race, for he knew that this must be—finally—the Wall of Devoir. He was almost there!

Covering his ears, against the roaring of the water, Jerol worked his way down to the river's edge, knelt down and dipped his hand through the churning current. Though the water looked as though it were boiling; it was cold as ice. It passed swiftly from his left to right. The water had a strange greenish tint but was so transparent he could see the streambed. Dancing webs of sunlight reflected from the river's bottom with each jumping wave. The riverbed was blanketed with smooth, mossy stones. Jerol had found the Green River.

The Ataraxia* glacier, high upon the Laodice* Mountains, feeds the lowland's unquenchable thirst for water. The ancient glacier had formed over hundreds of seasons of time and from this timeless mountain of melting ice flows the powerful currents of curiosity, imagination, and knowledge. If Jerol wanted to become a Blade, he would have to master their challenges.

Azrael would try to use the current's force to overwhelm Jerol. But if Jerol were successful, he would prove that he possesses what is required to become a Blade, someone who can transform curiosity, imagination, and knowledge into weapons of righteous war, weapons more powerful than the Dark Master's hideous plans to hold him down under the weight of the frigid water.

Jerol paced up and down the riverbank, impatiently searching for a way across. But all he found were the remnants of failed efforts of others who had come before. Stacks of stones, rotting ropes, and pieces of broken wood were scattered across the shore as far as he could see.

This was not going to be as simple as he had hoped. Jerol sat down on a dry spot, plugged his ears with beeswax, and began developing a plan. He peered up and down the river's banks, this time studying their dominant features. He noticed a pattern of rocky spots interspersed between wide stretches of beautiful, tan-colored soil. Jerol decided to move to a higher elevation where he could get an even better view. He climbed to the top of a boulder that stood about thirty hands above the water. The light from the sun was shining on the bluffs and face of the distant wall, creating waves of heat that were rising and disappearing in the clear blue sky. Because the shadows were beginning to point to the east, Jerol figured the time to be between midday and dusk.

The tired traveler decided to take a short nap, for he knew that a little rest would help him to make better decisions. So, he called Prayer and instructed him to fly watch while he settled down on the toasty, sun-baked rock and cleared his head.

The next thing Jerol remembered was waking up just as the sun was touching the distant treetops to the west. He had overslept. He barely had enough time to set up camp before nightfall. So, he hurriedly climbed down and started his search for a suitable spot. Luckily, he found just the place near the narrowest part of the river. Most of that night, he developed his plan for crossing the river by the light of his campfire.

It was late before Jerol retired for the night. The next day, he did not even stir from his dreams until midmorning. Confident that he had a good plan, he was in no hurry to get going and took plenty of time to eat a filling breakfast. That morning he splurged by fixing a pot of hot lentil soup simmered over a smoky fire. He roasted mint flower seeds and topped them with a spread of bubblebee honey. Bubblebees, a rare cross between honeybees and bumblebees, produced a scrumptious honey. Much to Jerol's delight, while taking a morning stroll by the river, he had stumbled upon a mature hive hidden in an old hollowed-out sugarhorn tree not far from camp. To wash the sweet syrup down, he had boiled river water the night before and left it to chill overnight in the river's icy waters. He ate as much as he could hold.

Jerol was ecstatic. If all went as planned, he would soon be bowing before the king!

Chapter 26

The Bridge

"Azrael had blocked my way with mounds of stone."
Logos 25:3:9

Jerol was content. Sometime during the previous night, a plan had come together in his dreams. He could not help but smile just thinking of its pure genius, for the plan was simple. He would get Prayer to carry him across. This would keep Jerol from risking life and limb in the unpredictable hands of the raging water. The plan was beautiful; he would sail across with little effort and arrive in Sentinel long before nightfall.

So, after enjoying a long breakfast, Jerol called for Prayer and told the curious bird of his brilliant idea. However, what Jerol thought would be an easy solution was not easy at all, for he quickly discovered that Prayer's behavior was beyond his control. Up to this point, Jerol thought that Prayer had been obedient to him. But, before long reality became painfully obvious, the bird had a mind of his own. (The truth was that Prayer responded only to a voice that Jerol could not hear. The

Royal falcon would only obey the voice of the King).

Standing next to the river, Jerol tried to coax his long-time friend. He even offered Prayer the bird's favorite treat, but Prayer remained stubbornly unwilling to co-operate. Jerol began to understand the Scroll's instruction: "When you ask, you do not receive, because you ask with wrong motives" (Logos 59:4:3). Prayer flew off, leaving Jerol bewildered and wondering what to do next. Much to his dismay, he would have to come up with another scheme.

So, after many more days of mulling over his situation, he came up with another idea. The first step required a small brick of soapstone.

On his earlier scouting hike, Jerol remembered spotting an outcropping of the oily stone near the outlet of a small spring. Several pieces had broken off and were lying partly hidden in the mud. Jerol quickly made his way back, scooped up a piece and began rubbing the blade of his sword across the stone's slick surface until each of its edges was razor sharp.

Armed with his newly honed sword, Jerol combed the jungle's edge for five medium-sized trees. They had to be straight and strong, about five hands wide, and tall enough to produce a pole that would be about twenty steps long.

Looking near the outlet of a creek that joined with the river, Jerol found a group of trees fitting his particular requirements. He chopped down five of the best and trimmed off their limbs leaving their abnormally rough bark intact. After finishing with the main trees, he then fashioned a smaller pole from a much younger tree. The pole was about half a hand wide and equal to Jerol's height. He used the new wooden rod to roll the five logs, one by one, down to the river. Jerol moved the pieces near the top of the riverbank in only a couple of days' time. Next he positioned each log end to end. Once in place, he carved notches around their ends and used vines to tie them together, making one long pole.

Standing on the riverbank, Jerol compared the length of his new bridge with the width of the river. According to his best guess, the new bridge would be just long enough to span from bank to bank. To his dismay, the sun quickly retreated behind the hills, forcing him to return to camp.

Early the next morning, the eager lad returned to his work and moved a few helmet-sized rocks down next to the channel's edge, then lined them up parallel to the river and about four steps apart. He walked back up to the top of the bank and began rolling his pole bridge back down the gentle slope until it came to rest upon the rocks. The primitive bridge lay parallel to the river's flow and about three steps from the water's edge.

Jerol's new plan was basic. First, he would stack enough rocks in front of and atop the downstream end of the pole bridge to prevent it from moving to the water. Then he would roll the upstream end into the current and, if everything went as planned, the long pole would be carried downstream until slamming against what appeared to be an outcropping of bedrock protruding from the opposite bank. His goal was to have a pole bridge floating on the river and anchored on one end by the rock pile and the other end by the outcropped rock. Jerol felt confident that the river's steady force would keep his bridge wedged tightly on the stone abutments, anchoring them down.

At last, his hard work was finished, and the time had come to test his plan. First, Jerol strategically anchored his waist to a nearby boulder to prevent being swept away should he lose his footing and fall into the churning water. With safety line in place, he slowly moved into the water and began guiding the loose end of his bridge into the rushing currents. Up close, the river's noise drowned out all other sound.

Jerol heaved the upstream end of the pole into the current; instantly he felt the power of the water's weight trying to twist him sideways. His feet began slipping on the slick stones of the riverbed! Even off balance, however, he was able to maneuver the bridge out and into the flow of the main current.

The bridge bounced and rocked violently in the churning water, accelerating down the river! Jerol was surprised to see how insignificant the bridge appeared when compared to the size of the great channel. The river would be another important test of Jerol's resourcefulness.

Would he be able to conquer the tricky currents of curiosity, imagination, and knowledge, or would he fail? Everywhere he looked lay evidence that constantly reminded him of the dashed hopes and dreams of countless others just like him. Some had been careless in their pursuit of Mettle's court and lost their lives to the river's cold, indifferent waters. Despite his fear, Jerol felt sure that he would prevail.

Jerol climbed back on shore just in time to watch the pole's free end slam against the protruding boulder on the other side. The bridge caught just as he had hoped! Jerol could hardly believe it. But, there it was—a long sturdy pole bridge stretching from one bank to the other! He held his breath and watched as the angry rapids pounded across his stubborn little bridge. The middle of the slender structure was bowing from the current's rage but was refusing to give up.

Confident that his bridge would hold, Jerol rushed back up the hill to gather his belongings. Suddenly, he was jolted by a loud snap followed by an even louder crack! He looked back just in time to watch in agony as his hopes began splintering apart! The bridge had snapped like a toothpick in the cruel hands of the mighty river! Jerol stood in stunned silence. What had taken him days to create had broken apart in mere moments.

Anguished and despairing, Jerol lumbered back to camp. He was cold, wet, and frustrated. He gathered dry sticks, started and stoked a fire into a steady blaze, and plopped down beside it. Glued down by discouragement, he stayed in the same spot for the rest of that day and night, wringing his sore, calloused hands; staring at the fire's comforting flames.

Twice he had been sure that victory was in his grasp only to face humiliation. Despondent and downcast, Jerol reluctantly surrendered to a nap in front of the soothing fire.

Chapter 27

Crossroad

"He trains my hand for battle; my arms can bend a bow of bronze." Logos 19:18:34

Jerol had reached a crossroad. He would conquer the river, or the river would conquer him. As far as he was concerned, failure was not an option. Again, he fished the Scrolls from his well-worn pack, for he was determined to study them until he found an answer. Days passed as he looked for inspiration. Then, one night, another idea appeared. It was like a message straight from the King. It would not be easy. There would be a lot more hard work to do, but he had a renewed confidence to try again.

To pull the design together, Jerol would have to travel back deeper into the jungle and search for another kind and particular size of tree. The size of the tree was to be about two hands wide, eighty hands tall and curved to the east. He looked for nearly three days before finding the perfect one. Wasting no time, he steadied himself, drew his sword and chopped until the stubborn tree dropped to the ground. Next, he stripped it of all bark and limbs. Recalling the skills he had used to craft the winning bow for his Bull's Eye match, Jerol whittled until the rough old tree began to take on the shape of a giant archer's bow. After seven days, he had finally completed it. About twice his height, the bow was sturdier than any he had ever held before! It presented a cylindrical handle about one hand thick, containing two flat roughened areas carved on its backside that anchored its middle. Jerol had crafted a mighty weapon!

Next, he focused his attention to making a suitable bowstring. Jerol extracted fibers from hand-selected vines and soaked them in a mixture of ash water, bee's wax and gypsum dust. After that, he tempered the strands by alternating them in baths of sunshine and the cold river for a couple of days. Then, lastly, he weaved the strands together into a super tough yet flexible string. The cord had a loop at each end and was slightly thicker in its middle. Prayer and Jerol had to work together to force the string onto the mighty bow. The bow straightened tight with a low humming sound. At last, the weapon was ready.

Without strong arrows, however, his efforts would be for naught. So, Jerol found and cut down three of the straightest oak saplings he could find and whittled them down into narrow shafts. They were almost as tall as him and as thick as two thumbs placed side by side.

He had chosen them for their balance between lightness and strength. Jerol held each of them up to his eye and bent them around his knee, checking their resistance, before choosing one of them.

From the straightest and toughest shaft, he fashioned his special arrow. For its point, he removed the whistle from his sword's handle and filed the silver pipe with river stones into a sharp point. He plied sharp barbs and hooks along its outer edges. To help keep the arrow on course, Jerol took a couple of Prayer's tail feathers, cut them to shape, and fastened them in slits etched about one full hand's width up from the butt end of the arrow. For his glue, he used a mixture of beeswax and animal fat. He then wound the feathers down tight with strands of thread from serpent vines. In a notch he had carved into the same end of the arrow, Jerol looped and firmly tied another special handmade rope. He had braided about one hundred steps worth of cord from the plentiful serpent vines that thrive along the riverbank. The rope was a half a thumb thick, lightweight, and strong.

At last Jerol's arsenal was ready. He spent the rest of the day firing test shots, fine-tuning his skills. He practiced until dusk. Then tired and satisfied, he retired back to camp. Making the bow, arrow, and rope had taken Jerol almost thirty days to complete. In only a few more days, he would execute the last part of his daring plan.

In final preparation he would rest for a few days, build his strength, and practice with his bow from sunup to sundown. This he did with a passion, until, one day he felt ready to face the River again.

Chapter 28

The Fording

"If anyone wishes to become a Blade, he must deny himself and conquer the fording."
Logos 40:16:24

The morning of the fording was gorgeous! Not a cloud was in the sky, and only a slight breeze stirred as Jerol readied his soul for battle. He closed his eyes, leaned back, and took a yawning breath, enjoying the clean smell of the moist river air. He felt the warmth of the sun's greeting caress his face. He would wait for the hottest part of the day before making his move, for the air would be at its thinnest then.

Jerol enjoyed his morning time with Prayer. He studied the great wall in the distance, a constant reminder of a task unfinished. He searched its surface through his looking glass until midday. He had hoped to spy Sentinel's great door, but the only thing he could see was the dark rugged, ivy-covered surface of the wall. For his final meal, Jerol scaled back from his usual portions, eating only a handful of royal jelly mixed with hazelnut oil.

Testing the direction and temperature of the wind, Jerol put his finger in his mouth, then held it up in the gentle breeze. The time had come. The air felt warm enough. Anxious to get started, he picked up his bow and arrow and slid down the slippery riverbank. He took his time and sat down behind three protruding rocks planted deeply in the ground. The two outer stones lay closest to the river's edge. He would anchor the soles of his feet on these outer rocks while pulling back on the bowstring.

The rocks were only a couple of steps from the water's edge. Jerol had not been this close to the river in several days. Its unfriendly roar brought back anxious feelings and uncomfortable memories of disappointment. But he forced them from his mind. If he were going to make it, he would have to stay focused. So, Jerol concentrated on the task at hand, placing the back of the bow's handle firmly on the riverside face of the center stone.

The awesome bow lay parallel to the ground. Jerol positioned its string behind his bent knees. He then laid his arrow on top of the handle and fitted its notch onto the thickened area of the string, which lay between his knees and just behind them. Prayer, who was perched close by, watched, tilting his head with curiosity. Jerol inspected the coils of rope beside him to make sure that it was secured to the arrow and the cords had not become tangled. The circular pile lay loosely on the ground, just as he had left it.

Across the rolling surface of the waters and shading the river was a mammoth tabor tree. The majestic timber resembled a huge black hand with an open and upturned palm reaching through the rich river soil, extending upward with its wrist at least twenty times higher than Jerol's head. Jerol could see Prayer sitting and sunning on the palm of the tree. The old tabor's solid trunk was half as wide as it was tall and offered an excellent target. The big tree would be hard to miss.

Finally, Jerol's list of checks was complete. The waiting was over. He was in position, sitting on the ground, with legs bent and leaning forward. First, he motioned Prayer out of the tree and back to camp. Once Prayer was clear of danger, he drew in a couple of slow deep breaths—the kind that fills your chest so full that it hurts a little. His eyes squinted with focused intensity, locking onto his target just across the river. He exhaled and took another full breath. This time he held the air in while straining with his upper body and slowly drawing back on the tightening string. He leaned back, placing his full weight into the pull. At the same time, he pushed forward with his legs, trying to straighten them. The bow's handle began tightening on the center stone. His plan was to bring as many muscles to bear as he could muster against the bow's stubborn resistance.

His face flushed beet red and froze in a twisted grimace. He gritted his teeth and pulled the string back as far as he could. His body began to shake from the stubborn resistance of the bow. The motion was compromising his ability to hold a steady aim. He was beginning to weaken and at the point of wanting to let go, when a most unexpected thing occurred.

Prayer moved in beside him and, using his beak, hooked the bowstring from between Jerol's hands! The powerful bird began back peddling in the dirt, digging his feet into the damp soil! The bow continued to flex backward!

Jerol sensed that the bow was about to reach its limit. Concerned that the string or the bow might break, he exhaled with a loud shout, "Release!" The great bow instantly recoiled, vibrating with a buzzing thud. Jerol snapped backwards, hitting his head on the soft ground, while Prayer tumbled back up the riverbank.

The sturdy shaft screamed above the waves, pulling behind it the rope that, if all went as planned, would serve as his lifeline. Before Jerol could right himself, the projectile had found its mark! But much to his dismay, the shot had not landed anywhere close to where he had hoped. Instead of hitting the tree's trunk, the arrow was embedded in a hefty root bulging about two hands up from the water's surface near the riverbank.

Jerol's heart sank. He might have to go back again to the drawing board. He quickly pulled his spyglass out to take a closer look. The arrow was near the center of the tree and buried deeply enough into the tabor's stubborn wood to hide its barbed tip. If the barbs were fully engaged, there was hope that he would still be able to use it!

Jerol heard a rustling noise on the ground nearby. He followed the sound to the coil of rope that was quickly unraveling. He sprang to his feet and ran for the rope. Its middle was in the water, being rapidly carried downstream and away from him. He reached into the unwinding coil to stop its escape and yanked the rope back out of the river's greedy clutches. He retracted the cord; hand over hand, until the line was taut. He then wrapped it five times around and tied it to a nearby tree. When he was done, the rope line stretched across the channel at a slight angle.

Because the arrow had landed so low in the tabor's roots, most of the rope lay just under the water's surface. Jerol's original plan had counted on the rope being dry and about twenty hands above the water.

He should have been half the way across the river. Instead, he was wondering how the rope would perform while wet. So, to test its strength, he unwrapped the line from the tree, and began pulling it. Prayer instinctively joined in.

Jerol leaned back, peddling hard, trying not to lose his footing. Prayer began working his feet into the mud, and pushing the air with his powerful wings. The big bird was focused so intently on pulling, that he was not paying much attention to Jerol and almost knocked him into the water!

The boy scrambled out of Prayer's way and lay low on the ground as the powerful falcon jerked with increasing force. Jerol watched in amazement as the top of the giant tabor began to shake. The rope was unbelievably strong and more than sufficient. Jerol was convinced; the arrow and rope would not fail!

Still pinned to the ground, Jerol waved his arms. Prayer let go of the line. Jerol jumped up, chased the rope, and snatched it before it could slip back into the river. He then carefully looped the cord several times back around the tree and retied the slippery line with three knots.

At last, Jerol could collect his belongings and prepare for the crossing. He pushed the Scrolls down deep into a sheepskin pouch. He had sewn the bag with its wool to the inside and leather to the outside. The unique construction provided the best protection from the elements. Jerol stitched the top together and then enclosed the entire bag with a generous coating of beeswax. "This will keep the Scrolls dry," he thought.

His bedding, eating utensils, and other belongings had each been wrapped the night before and placed in his main backpack. Jerol also covered the sack with a generous coating of molten wax. Jerol figured that the best way to get the heavy armor to the other side of the river was to wear it. So, after securing his baggage, he put on his body armor. Testing for looseness, he tugged on all of the armor's belts and straps. Once his armor was firmly strapped down, he attached the backpack to his body by tightly wrapping it with freshly cut vines tied around his chest and stomach. He pulled and tugged on his gear until satisfied that it was river proof.

With nothing left to check, Jerol lumbered down to the river's edge, clanking with each step. Anxious to see the King, he did not hesitate, but instead grabbed the line and splashed through the bone-chilling water! The noise of the river seemed to double as he walked into its grasp. The frigid water bit down hard, quickly revealing the reality of danger. Jerol would have to move quickly if he were to have hope of making it. Hand over hand he began pulling farther out and into the roiling water.

Within moments the water level rose up and covered his chest. The icy undercurrents cut across his legs trying hard to force his feet out from under him! Jerol thought he had prepared for every possible situation, but this was proving much more difficult than he had imagined. He was becoming waterlogged at an alarming rate. The force of the rushing water was pushing, shoving, and twisting him without mercy!

Jerol showed no fear and held on with a stubborn

grip. The angry water tried repeatedly to tear his hands free of the line. But he refused to let go. From the roar of the water came a sound like voices warning him to go back! He forced the thought from his mind, recalling that one of the main sayings of the Logos taught that "no one who puts his hand to the plow and looks back is fit for service in the kingdom" (Logos 42:9:62). So, more determined than ever, he continued throwing one hand in front of the other, bit-by-bit making his way through the buffeting torrents.

Remarkably, Jerol had somehow clamored to within about twenty steps of the opposite riverbank! However, his fight with the river was taking a dangerous toll. His strength was fading fast. The bitter cold and constant push of the river were hammering him like two prize-fighters landing alternating blows to his freezing, weary body. He was having difficulty feeling his unprotected legs. For the first time, he began to doubt that he would make it.

Knowing that he was too weak to turn back, the brave boy lowered his head and did the only thing he knew how to do: move forward! He was past the point of no return! Jerol remembered how, in Malevolence, he had gotten the key of courage, not by running away, but by standing firm against the deluge of slander and gossip, and how the sword had delivered him when everything else had collapsed around him.

So, Jerol decided to stop struggling with the river. He released his right hand and held on with his left. He pushed his right arm down through the water feeling for his trusty sword. The current slapped hard along the sword, trying to rip the icy metal from his weakening grip. For a moment the hateful current pushed the sword downstream, pressing Jerol's right arm tightly onto his side. Answering the challenge, Jerol forced the sword up and then out of the water's churning surface, pointing its blade straight up toward the sky!

The swirling water flipped him around until he was lying face down. His body stretched out parallel with the river bottom. The tremendous force of the current held his entire body under the water's surface, keeping him from rising up and catching a breath! By now, his right arm was fully extended. He struggled to grip the bouncing line with his left hand. The feeble rope was his last connection to hope. In a remarkable show of stubborn will, Jerol kept the sword up and out of the water's ragged surface!

Even though he tried to hold on with every ounce of determination, the boy was totally spent and his strength was gone. The numbing water had bludgeoned away most of his resolve, and he was struggling just to hold on! All of a sudden, the hateful river let out a cruel roar, slamming an extra surge of weight into him, this time ripping his frozen fingers free from the slippery cord. In an instant my courageous son had become just another piece of floating debris, helpless and subject to the river's shifting moods.

Jerol felt afraid and alone. He was helpless and powerless. Now he could do nothing but ride the merciless rapids. Then, when it seemed that things could not get any worse, he was jolted by something slamming into him from behind! The force pushed him deeper under the water. He feared that he might hit the bottom. Jerol

rotated his heavy head, and, through the haze of the water's white-capped surface, he caught a glimpse of something large out of the corner of his eye.

It was Prayer! The boy's best friend was fighting the air and water with his awesome wings and tugging with all his might! Jerol could feel his body being pulled through and out of the river's frosty grip. He coughed and gasped for air! His vision began to blur; time seemed to stop. Then, everything turned to darkness.

Jerol felt something warm on his cheek. He longed to wake up and run from his chilly nightmare and into the warmth. Slowly he cracked opened his heavy eyes. From ground level he could see Prayer sitting only ten steps away, with wings spread wide, basking in the hot sun.

As soon as he saw his friend, Jerol knew he was not dreaming! The battered boy eased up and onto his aching arms. He was stiff and sore, especially in his shoulders, proof that his fight with the river had been real. Somehow, he was alive and sitting on the Sentinel side of the riverbank! He sat up and looked to his left to find the river's edge only twenty steps away.

About thirty steps away to his right was an orchard of beautiful firefan trees covering the forest floor and growing underneath a stand of ancient tabors. The old trees were evenly spaced, standing like pillars in a scared temple. Jerol twisted his upper body and looked back across the river. He was surprised to find his rope still bending with the river's flow. At that instant, he could feel in his bones that his journey was about to end.

He stood up, scraped the green moss and mud from his arms and legs, and checked his armor. Every piece was accounted for and undamaged! He scanned the area for his backpack and found the wrinkled bag just a few steps away. Jerol was happy to find that his baggage had remained intact! A tiny amount of water had compromised the seal, but nothing was harmed.

Jerol looked back at Prayer. Through tears of joy, he saw a shiny object hanging from the bird's beautiful neck! Hoping that the item might be the final key, he ran to Prayer and lifted the trinket to his eyes. Yes! He had found the last key! It was the key of VISION! Because he had used the Scrolls and dreamed of a plan, persevered with courage, and overcome the wild river currents, Jerol had demonstrated vision. In his excitement and joy, he tried to embrace Prayer, nearly knocking him off his feet. "Thank you, my friend, for saving my life!" he cried.

Eager to finish the quest, Jerol pulled at his faithful ally and exclaimed, "Come on, boy. Let's go find the door! I'm anxious to use these keys that we've worked so hard to find!" Prayer leapt into the air with a victory cry and disappeared above the trees. Jerol gathered up his things, placed the key next to the others on the ring of his sword, and then disappeared into the shadows of the forest walking as fast as he could in the direction of the great wall.

As he walked he pondered the lesson of that day—a lesson that would change him forever. He had discovered that whenever life gets tough and he does not think that he can go on, he would not give up. Instead, he would keep pushing, keep trying, and, even if his strength gave out, he would trust in Prayer's ability to see him through.

Chapter 29

The Door

"He said to me, 'Son of man, now dig into the wall.' So I dug into the wall and saw a doorway there."
Logos 26:8:8

As you may recall from the first chapter of my story, the first time we met Jerol was shortly before he had reached Sentinel's wall. Nighttime had fallen and Jerol was approached by Azrael, cleverly disguised as a beautiful angel of light. Once Azrael's true identity was revealed, however, the Dark Lord summoned his minion Sin to attack. The demon swine assailed, but was stopped in his tracks by Prayer, who quickly removed and dispensed of the squealing imp. Alone, Jerol and Azrael squared off in a fierce battle where Jerol had found an opening to strike. Yet, instead of landing the decisive blow, the eager boy lost his footing, cracked his head upon a rock, and was knocked unconscious. And with the mighty Ruler of Darkness just steps away and my son lying helpless upon the ground, Jerol's Crossing was in serious jeopardy.

Jerol slowly opened his eyes. His ears were ringing and he did not know where he was. He looked up and saw Azrael, with his back to the wall, towering above him like a hungry bear perched over its helpless prey. The old dragon threw back his head and began laughing. "How stupid you are, little one. You are no match for me! Your end is near!"

Jerol lay just steps away from the cliff's edge. Even though still unsteady from his fall, he managed to ignore the threats and stay focused on the task at hand. Mentally, he screamed at his aching body "Move!" Jerol knew if he remained immobile for one more instant the battle would be over. He felt a surge of power move through his weary limbs like he had never felt before! Somehow, he began moving, not in his strength, but with the authority of the King! Buying precious time and dodging with blinding speed, the courageous boy evaded Azrael's grasp and rolled out from under the stomping beast.

Showing no fear, he leapt to his feet, spun to face his enemy and lunged forward with all his might, pushing his trusted weapon up at Azrael's bobbing head. As the sharp, sturdy blade parted the air, a great clap of thunder cracked out followed by a blast of searing heat!

The sky flashed with uneven lightning bolts streaking in at Jerol from the horizon. The maze of bolts slammed together at a point directly above Jerol's head, creating the sound of an avalanche and a spectacular display of lights. The radiance briefly collected in a voluminous spinning fireball fifteen steps across, but then rapidly began compressing into a small, dense sphere of solid light almost metallic in appearance. Azrael had waited too long to retreat and was backed up on the wall. He was so taken by the noise and light show that he did not see the approaching blade!

Just as the sword met with Azrael's thick neck, the molten ball exploded upward in a vibrating stream of liquid flame! The glowing stream of molten metal blasted skyward and ripped through the base of the clouds. The churning clouds above looked as though fire was trapped between their walls. Brilliant flashes of light appeared to be furiously punching into the billows, trying to get out. Suddenly, an immense blue blaze blew out through the bottom of the clouds. The fire streamed from the heavens and onto the sword, engulfing Azrael from head to toe! The burning dragon gagged and cried out in torment. He reeled and rocked violently, and then with tremendous force slammed into the wall, causing an explosion which burst out in a shower of broken rock before retreating back into the forest.

Jerol crashed to his knees and bunched up behind his

shield. Once the debris had stopped falling, he quickly looked up and watched the light from the Evil Ruler's burning form grow dim until his charred carcass disappeared back into the darkness of the woods. Could it be? Had he defeated Azrael once and for all? Jerol knew that he must not tarry long to find out. He needed to quickly make his way into the city, for he would surely find safety there.

Once satisfied that he was no longer in immediate danger, Jerol turned back to face the wall. Where Azrael had stood, Jerol could see the outline of a door buried in the shadows behind a pile of broken rock. He climbed up onto the rubble and reached back with his arm, swiping his hand across the door's flat surface. The clean trail left by his hand revealed a swash of sparkling gold!

It became clear that Azrael had been trying to hide this particular door from the boy's view. Jerol reasoned that the massive slab must be the main door to Sentinel! One by one he removed the pieces of rubble until he had uncovered the entire door. Pulling bedding from his backpack, he wiped down the door until he was able to see his reflection.

Up high, near the top of the door, Jerol could see giant letters etched into its golden face. They were the four words he had longed to see: SENTINEL—CITY OF DESTINY! However, the next thing he saw were three small, snarling and hissing demons hugging the locks at each corner of the door. They were dark with eyes burning like bright red rubies. Jerol quickly assessed the situation. The locks looked like molten metal that had been quickly cooled with ice water. They looked rough and irregular in shape. And, the keyholes appeared to be well guarded by various rusty and sharp metal barbs covered with a black, greasy liquid. He recognized the slime to be nightshade, one of the most deadly poisons of Sheol.

Jerol stood his ground, stared into the demons glowing eyes and shouted. "I have just defeated Azrael, the mighty Ruler of the Damned. You imps will be child's play!" Undeterred, he drew his sword and quickly gathered the four special keys from its hilt ring.

Holding his sword ready with his left hand, Jerol cautiously handled the only unguarded lock with his right hand, trying to avoid the barbs and slime. But, Qualm was hiding, crouched in the shadow of the latch and was holding tightly to its sides with his hind feet. Seeking to startle Jerol, the sprite reached around with each hand and started grabbing at the key. Surprised, Jerol jumped back. When he did, he dropped the key, which fell directly into the spindly claws of Qualm! There was a loud pop and a bright flash of light. Astonished, Jerol stood in silence. The key lay on the ground, but the hideous scamp was nowhere to be found! Shaken by the realization that the keys possessed Royal power, Fear, Apathy and Chicane leapt screaming from the door and jumped in terror off the edge of the cliff!

Wasting no time, Jerol inserted the key of VISION and unlatched the lock with one turn. He grabbed the lock once guarded by Fear, inserted the key of COURAGE, and quickly released it from the wall! The third lock was the lock of Chicane. Jerol fetched the key of INTEGRITY and freed the third lock. Finally, only one remained—the lock of Apathy! With the key of SERVICE he unlatched the final lock! Sentinel was just one step away!

Jerol pushed and leaned hard into the door. The giant panel began to pop and crack, creeping forward! He stepped back and watched as the solid, heavy door slowly swung inward. He stood breathless, wide-eyed, gazing in anticipation. The door drifted open revealing a road made of translucent blue stones leading to a beautiful city of dancing lights! Sentinel appeared to be around one thousand steps to the east. Jerol could see streets that were shiny and white, the buildings bright and crystal clear. He could see waves of heat rising from great transparent monuments. Tall glass-like structures pierced the sky like giant shards of diamond! "At last, the place where I can become everything King Deus wants me to be. One day, my wife and I will raise our family here. On manhood's court I will work and serve my King and fellow man." Jerol reflected.

He closed his eyes then took a satisfying breath; the air smelled clean and fresh, like the breeze does after a steady rain. He cleaned and straightened his armor, crossed the threshold through Devoir*, and entered the sacred city!

Much to his surprise, Jerol's mother and I were waiting just inside the gate to greet him. After the boys left Gelandesprung, Charity and I traveled back to Sentinel where we had been waiting for their arrival. Recently, Prayer had notified us that Jerol was nearing the city. We had been camped out near the doorway for a few days.

We held on to our son as though we would never let go! We laughed and cried for joy, expressing our delight and pleasure in his great accomplishment. Our beloved Jerol was a true man. Soon he would receive the Mark of the Blade!

He had learned how to repel the pain of unkindness, to overcome the selfishness of greed, and to show self-control when tempted by unhealthy pleasures. He had developed a plan for dealing with the Green River and its currents of untamed curiosity, imagination, and knowledge, and, above everything, he had conquered the false security of his pride. By overcoming these, he had shown to be a capable warrior, and by resisting Azrael's temptations, he had proved his loyalty to the King.

How important it is for you to know that his victories came from one source—his daily trust in and submission to the Logos! His faith in its guidance had unleashed the power of Paladin who, in one form or another, had always come to his aid! Without the Logos, Jerol would have faced each test in his power and been defeated just like his brother Jadan. Yet, through obedience he had shown courage, integrity, service, and vision —the means to becoming a true man, the keystones of the Mettle's mark.

Arm in arm we walked away from the open doorway to the heart of the city. Once there, Jerol would receive the objects of his quest—the Mark of the Blade and a place at the King's table!

Jerol was ready. Ready to face the future. Ready to serve the King for the rest of his days. At last, his Crossing was complete; the quest for manhood was done.

Epilogue

"When I was a child, I talked like a child, I thought like a child, I reasoned like a child. When I became a man, I put childish ways behind me" LOGOS 46:13:11

You might be wondering what Jadan's and Jerol's lives are like today. Jadan did not escape the angry Bigots, was recaptured, and was held captive for several more summers. Once his wounds healed, he was able to make a lucky, daring escape. But, instead of heading to Sentinel, he made his way back to Sophistdale. And to this day he continues to roam the land of Adulthood with a group of Preeners.

On rare occasions, we visit him. I sense he is lonely. He acts as though he is doing fine, but I can tell that his smile is just an act. That's Jadan—always the actor. As for a family, he has been married three times. But, each relationship has been wrecked by his self-centered attitude.

Whenever I get the opportunity, I still encourage him to read the Scrolls and not give up on finding manhood, but he says that he is too busy. I am afraid Jadan will come to the end of his life as an unhappy, unfulfilled person—an adult, but not a true man. I am saddened when thinking about how, because of his choices, his life is so full of needless misery. But, he must decide how he wants to live. I have done all that I can do.

As for Jerol, he has been prospering for the past fourteen summers. He serves on the court of Mettle and two summers ago, he was honored as an Elder Blade. To be an Elder Blade is to have the highest honor given by the court. Some days he stands guard near the Wall of Devoir. Other days he travels throughout the regions of Terrenea waging war against Azrael and the Netherworld.

The same summer that he entered Sentinel, Jerol sent Prayer back to Éclat to find Grace. Four summers later they were married. Jerol and Grace currently live in Gelandesprung where they are raising three feisty sons of their own: Troth*, Languor*, and Ardor*. In fact, my grandsons are the main reason for sharing this story. This year will bring Troth's turn to leave Gelandesprung for his Crossing.

It would not be the truth if I said all has gone perfectly for Jerol and Grace. They have seen their share of disappointment and heartbreak along the way. They still suffer from iniquity's touch and get sick from time to time. But they trust the wisdom of the Logos to guide them each day. They have learned that staying in favor with the King gives them a peace they cannot understand. And their joy far exceeds their sorrow.

So, how exactly do you enter the courts of Mettle? A few important lessons can be learned from Jerol's success and Jadan's failure.

First, you must possess the gift of the prince and make your vow of submission.

Second, you must strive to correctly apply the teaching of the Logos to each circumstance in which you find yourself.

Third, be disciplined in studying the Scrolls combined with daily communications with the King. This will keep you on track and ready to face your opponents.

Fourth, make extra effort each day to put on your full armor.

Fifth, become skilled in the use of your sword.

Sixth, do not trust in your own power, but in the King's provision instead.

And last, you must have the four foundational character traits of those who sit on Mettle's court, from which the keys were drawn: courage, integrity, service, and vision.

The successful application of these elements paved the way into manhood and the Mark for Jerol and can be summed up in four words—obedience to the King.

I hope that hearing about Jadan and Jerol's crossing will help you to find your way to manhood. Just like them, you must choose which road you will take.

Choose wisely.

Glossary

Glossary definitions are taken from one of the five sources listed below. The source is indicated by the superscript number.

1. *word goes here.* Dictionary.com. *Dictionary.com Unabridged* (v 1.1). Random House, Inc. http://dictionary.reference.com/browse/WORD GOES HERE (accessed: January 07, 2007).

2. *word goes here.* Dictionary.com. *WordNet® 2.1.* Princeton University. http://dictionary.reference.com/browse/ WORD GOES HERE (accessed: January 07, 2007).

3. *word goes here.* Dictionary.com. *The American Heritage® Dictionary of the English Language, Fourth Edition.* Houghton Mifflin Company, 2004. http://dictionary.reference.com/browse/ WORD GOES HERE (accessed: January 07, 2007).

4. *word goes here.* Dictionary.com. *The American Heritage® Stedman's Medical Dictionary.* Houghton Mifflin Company. http://dictionary.reference.com/browse/ WORD GOES HERE (accessed: January 07, 2007).

Places (See Map)

Agog[1]- highly excited by eagerness, curiosity, anticipation, etc.
Ataraxia[1]- a state of freedom from emotional disturbance and anxiety; tranquility.
Backbiter[1] (Mountains)- someone who attacks the character or reputation of a person who is not present.
Belle[1]-a woman or girl admired for her beauty and charm.
Black[1] (Mountains)- boding ill; sullen or hostile; threatening: *black words; black looks*
Bravura[2]- brilliant and showy technical skill
Callow[1]- immature or inexperienced
Covet[1] (on)- to desire wrongfully, inordinately, or without due regard for the rights of others: *to covet another's property.*
Daunt[1]- to lessen the courage of; dishearten
Éclat[3]- Great brilliance, as of performance or achievement.
Élan[1] (Creek)- Ardor inspired by passion or enthusiasm
Eos[1]- the ancient Greek goddess of the dawn
Euphoria[4]- a feeling of great happiness or well-being, commonly exaggerated and not necessarily well-founded
Eye[1]- to fix the eyes upon; view
Foison[1]- abundance; plenty
Gall[1]- something bitter or severe
Gelandesprung[1]- a jump, usually over an obstacle, in which one plants both poles in the snow in advance of the skis, bends close to the ground, and propels oneself chiefly by the use of the poles
Gevah - Hebrew transliteration - pride, a lifting up
Graven[2] (wood)- cut into a desired shape; "graven images;" "sculptured representations"
Greed[1]- excessive or rapacious desire, esp. for wealth or possessions
Ichor[1]- *Classical Mythology.* an ethereal fluid flowing in the veins of the gods.

Laodice - Church in Laodicea: Assembly of believers that Jesus expressed extreme displeasure in. See Revelation 3:16.

Lode[1]- a rich supply or source.

Malevolence[1]- the quality, state, or feeling of being malevlolent; ill will; malice; hatred.

Mammon[1]- *New Testament.* riches or material wealth. Matt. 6:24; Luke 16:9,11,13.

Miriam[1] (City)- a female given name, form of Mary

(Mount) Hecatomb[1]- any great slaughter

(Mount) Sheol[1]- the abode of the dead or of departed spirits

(Mountains of) Maiden[1]- a girl or young unmarried woman; maid

(Mountains of) Mirth[1]- amusement or laughter

Narcissa - Narcissism[1]: inordinate fascination with oneself; excessive self-love; vanity

Rancor[1]- bitter, rankling resentment or ill will; hatred; malice

(Sea of) Plethora[1]- overabundance; excess

Sentinel[1]-a soldier stationed as a guard to challenge all comers and prevent a surprise attack:

Seraph[1] (ic) - having a sweet nature befitting an angel or cherub.

Shylock[1]- a hard-hearted moneylender

Sophist[1] (dale)- a person who reasons adroitly and speciously rather than soundly

Swivet[1] - a state of nervous excitement, haste, or anxiety; flutter

Tremulous[1] (Mountains)- of persons, the body, etc. characterized by trembling, as from fear, nervousness, or weakness.

Terrenea - the earth.

Obdurate[1]- stubbornly resistant to moral influence; persistently impenitent

Perfidy[1]- an act or instance of faithlessness or treachery

Palaestral[1]- a public place for training or exercise in wrestling or athletics.

Vestal[1] (River)- of, pertaining to, or characteristic of a vestal virgin; chaste; pure

Wistful[1]- characterized by melancholy; longing; yearning

Kingdom of Light (Royal Race and The Eternal Souls)

Ardor[1]- intense devotion, eagerness, or enthusiasm; zeal
Charity[1]- Christian love; agape.
Devoir[1]- something for which a person is responsible; duty
Gerhorsam - German word for obedience.
Grace[1]- the freely given, unmerited favor and love of God
Helmet - And take the helmet of salvation, and the sword of the Spirit, which is the Word of God, (Eph 6:17) Modern King James Translation
Jerol(in) - holy
Keys[1]- something that affords a means of access
King (Deus[1])- God
Languor[1]- lack of spirit or interest
Lector[1]- a lecturer in a college or university
Logos[1]- the divine word or reason incarnate in Jesus Christ. John 1:1–14.
Lyrics[1]- (of poetry) having the form and musical quality of a song
Magic[1](al) – mysteriously enchanting: *a magical night*
Prayer[1]- a spiritual communion with God or an object of worship, as in supplication, thanksgiving, adoration, or confession. Also, a petition; entreaty.
Pantheon[1]- heroes
(Prince) Paladin[1]- any determined advocate or defender of a noble cause.
Psalm[1] (ists)-a sacred song or hymn
Psalter[1]- a psalmbook
Rue[1]- pity or compassion
Sanguine[1]- cheerfully optimistic, hopeful, or confident
Seine[1]- to fish for or catch with a seine

Shield - Above all, take the shield of faith, with which you shall be able to quench all the fiery darts of the wicked. (Eph 6:16) Modern King James Translation

Sword - And take the helmet of salvation, and the sword of the Spirit, which is the Word of God, (Eph 6:17) Modern King James Translation

Tenets[2] - a religious doctrine that is proclaimed as true without proof [syn: *dogma*]

Troth[1]- faithfulness, fidelity, or loyalty

Vicar[3] - a person who acts in place of another; substitute.

Way of Light[1]- spiritual illumination or awareness; enlightenment

Xeno[4]- Stranger; foreigner

The Shadow Kingdom (The Damned)

Addiction[1]- the condition of being habitually or compulsively occupied with or involved in something.

Azrael[1]- the angel who separates the soul from the body at the moment of death.

Bacchus[1]- the god of wine; Dionysus

Badger[1] (winds)- to harass or urge persistently; pester; nag

Jadan - foolish (resulting from or showing a lack of sense; ill-considered)

Black Henbane[2] - poisonous fetid Old World herb having sticky hairy leaves and yellow-brown flowers (used in this story to represent hate)

Brawl[1] (er)- a noisy quarrel, squabble, or fight.

Candor[3] - the state or quality of being frank, open, and sincere in speech or expression; candidness: *The candor of the speech impressed the audience.*

Chicane[1] - deception; chicanery

Chthon[1]- idolater

Coal - represents an attitude of apathy.

Covet[1] - to desire wrongfully, inordinately, or without due regard for the rights of others.

Curule[1]- of the highest rank.

Delilah[1]- a seductive and treacherous woman.

Eidolon[1]- a phantom; apparition

Envy[1] - a feeling of discontentment or covetousness with regard to another's advantages, success, possessions, etc.

Ergot[1] - a disease of rye and other cereal grasses (used in this story to represent violence)

Fetter[1]- *Usually, fetters.* anything that confines or restrains

Fetter-Debt[1]- something that is owed or that one is bound to pay to or perform for another

Gascon[1]- boastful; bragging

Greenstone - represents an attitude of doubt.

Hedonism[1]- the doctrine that pleasure or happiness is the highest good

Hellion[1]- a disorderly, troublesome, rowdy, or mischievous person.

Huckster[1]- a persuasive and aggressive salesperson.

Huckster - Chabal- Hebrew transliteration - to take a pledge, lay to pledge

Huckster-Daneion - Greek transliteration - a loan

Huckster-Kleros - Greek transliteration - an object used in casting or drawing lots, which was either a pebble, or a potsherd, or a bit of wood

Iniquity[2]- absence of moral or spiritual values; "the powers of darkness"

Iron – represents an attitude of fear

Jezebel - *(often lowercase)* a wicked, shameless woman.

Larkspur – a plant poison (used in this story to represent flattery)

Lightgames - Video games

Locks[1]- a contrivance for fastening or securing something.

Lust[1]- a passionate or overmastering desire or craving (usually fol. by for): a lust for power.

Lyrics-(Preeners[1]**)** - to pride (oneself) on an achievement, personal quality, etc.:

Lyrics-Preener-Dirge1- the office of the dead

Mettle[1] (spirit)- disposition or temperament

Sin[3]- An evil. (Sin -Deliberate disobedience to the known will of God.)

Okneros - Greek transliteration – slothful, lazy

Opiates[1]- Something that dulls the senses and induces relaxation or torpor.

Pernicious[1]- deadly; fatal

Qualm[1] - a sudden feeling of apprehensive uneasiness; misgiving

Red Squill[1] - a variety of squill whose bulbs are red, used chiefly as a rat poison. (used in this story to represent lies)

Sabaist[1]- idolater

Selfs-Bigots[1]- a person who is utterly intolerant of any differing creed, belief, or opinion

Selfs-Heinous[1]- hateful; odious; abominable; totally reprehensible

Selfs-(Puff[1]**)er**- to inflate with pride, vanity, etc.

Seraph[1] - having a sweet nature befitting an angel or cherub.

Slander[1] - a malicious, false, and defamatory statement or report.

Spirits[1] (drugs) - *Often, spirits.* a strong distilled alcoholic liquor.

Traprock - represents an attitude of distrust.

Sunstone - video devices (i.e. Television, Internet, etc.)

The Four Keys Of Mettle (Manhood)

Vision

(Dream God's plan.)

"Where there is no vision, the people perish." Proverbs 29:18

Courage

(Pursue your dream and never give up)

"Have I not commanded you? Be strong and courageous. Do not be terrified; do not be discouraged, for the Lord your God will be with you wherever you go." Joshua 1:9

Integrity

(All your thoughts, words, and actions—God's way not yours)

"I know, my God, that you test the heart and are pleased with integrity." I Chronicles 29:17

Service

(Use your personal resources to serve God and people)

"Love the Lord your God with all your heart and with all your soul and with all your strength and with all your mind; and, Love your neighbor as yourself." Luke 10:27

____

____

____

How To Become A Modern Day Blade (True Man)

1. Agree with Jesus that you have not always done things His way.
2. Ask Him to forgive you.
3. Trust Him with your present and future.
4. Seek to do all things His way and not your own.
5. Read His Books and talk with Him often.
6. Take part in a Christ-centered church.

For more clarity, go to His Books (the Bible) and read the following Scriptures:

- For all have sinned and come short of the glory of God. (Rom 3:23)
- For the wages of sin is death, but the gift of God is eternal life through Jesus Christ our Lord. (Rom 6:23)
- And leading them outside, he said, Sirs, what must I do to be saved? And they said, Believe on the Lord Jesus Christ and you shall be saved, and your household. (Act 16:30-31)
- For God so loved the world that He gave His only-begotten Son, that whoever believes in Him should not perish but have everlasting life. (John 3:16)
- Because if you confess the Lord Jesus, and believe in your heart that God has raised Him from the dead, you shall be

saved. (Rom 10:9)

- For by grace you are saved through faith, and that not of yourselves, it is the gift of God, not of works, lest anyone should boast. (Eph 2:8-9)
- You are the light of the world. A city that is set on a hill cannot be hidden. Nor do men light a lamp and put it under the grain-measure, but on a lampstand. And it gives light to all who are in the house. Let your light so shine before men that they may see your good works and glorify your Father who is in Heaven. (Mat 5:14-16)
- And, behold, a certain lawyer stood up and tempted Him, saying, Master, what shall I do to inherit eternal life? He said to him, What is written in the Law? How do you read it? And answering, he said, You shall love the Lord your God with all your heart, and with all your soul, and with all your strength, and with all your mind, and your neighbor as yourself. And He said to him, You have answered right; do this and you shall live. (Luke 10:25-28)
- Your Word is a lamp to my feet, and a light to my path. (Psa 119:105)
- And let us consider one another to provoke to love and to good works, not forsaking the assembling of ourselves together, as the manner of some is, but exhorting one another, and so much the more as you see the Day approaching. (Heb 10:24-25)
- And they were continuing steadfastly in the apostles' doctrine, and in fellowship and in the breaking of the loaves, and in prayers. (Act 2:42)

Gerhorsam (vow of submission), as described in the story, represents participation in a real life ceremony called baptism. Some very smart people believe that this ceremony is needed for salvation. Other smart people believe it is not. One thing is clear,

God desires for everyone who is a part of his Kingdom, and is physically able to be baptized. In my opinion, water baptism is an announcement—"Hey everybody, look what God did! He's changed me from a walking dead man (spiritually speaking) to a new creature that will live forever! Because of who He is and the unbelievable gift He's given to me, I plan to follow Him the rest of my days!" Submission to God's desires is a must for true manhood. Please search the Bible and make your own conclusions about the importance of baptism.

- Therefore we were buried with Him by baptism into death, so that as Christ was raised up from *the* dead by the glory of the Father; even so we also should walk in newness of life. (Rom 6:4)

Putting on your spiritual armor daily will allow you to live more successfully as a true man.

- Put on the whole armor of God so that you may be able to stand against the wiles of the devil. For we do not wrestle against flesh and blood, but against principalities, against powers, against the world's rulers, of the darkness of this age, against spiritual wickedness in high *places*. Therefore take to yourselves the whole armor of God, that you may be able to withstand in the evil day, and having done all, to stand. Therefore stand, having your loins girded about with truth, and having on the breastplate of righteousness and your feet shod with the preparation of the gospel of peace. Above all, take the shield of faith, with which you shall be able to quench all the fiery darts of the wicked. And take the helmet of salvation, and the sword of the Spirit, which is the Word of God, praying always with all prayer and supplication in the Spirit, and watching to this very thing with all perseverance and supplication for all saints. (Eph 6:11-18)

Reflections of the Blade

Use the following guide to go deeper into the lessons of Sentinel.

Chapter 1- The Offering

Like Jerol's struggle with Azrael, so is your life and mine. On earth it's a battle between good and evil … between us and an enemy who is out to keep us from following King Jesus.

Finally, my brethren, be strong in the Lord and in the power of His might. Put on the whole armor of God, that you may be able to stand against the wiles of the devil. For we do not wrestle against flesh and blood, but against principalities, against powers, against the rulers of the darkness of this age, against spiritual hosts of wickedness in the heavenly places. (Ephesians 6:10-12)

- Can you see the battle going on around you? List some things you experience at home, school or work that would be evidence of such a battle:

____

____

____

Ponder points: Why would we need prisons if there were not evil at work on earth? Why are there wars raging upon the earth if evil is not at work?

Chapter 2- Bull's Eye

When thinking about the contest, did Jadan and Jerol approach the challenge the same way?

- List how Jadan approached his turn:

- List how Jerol approached his turn:

- Which way produced the best outcome and why?

Chapter 3- The Gift

Just like the Terreneans were poisoned by iniquity, you and I have been poisoned by the sin of Adam and Eve in the garden of Eden.

Then the Lord God said, "Behold, the man has become like one of Us, to know good and evil. And now, lest he put out his hand and take also of the tree of life, and eat, and live forever"-- therefore the Lord God sent him out of the garden of Eden to till the ground from which he was taken. So He drove out the man; and He placed cherubim at the east of the garden of Eden, and a flaming sword which turned every way, to guard the way to the tree of life. (Genesis 3:22-24)

For all have sinned and come short of the glory of God. (Rom 3:23)

For the wages of sin is death, but the gift of God is eternal life through Jesus Christ our Lord. (Rom 6:23)

- If God warns us about the consequences of our behavior and we disregard that warning, what should we expect to happen?

____

____

____

____

For God so loved the world that He gave His only begotten Son, that whoever believes in Him should not perish but have everlasting life. (John 3:16)

- Just like the Terrenean's only cure for iniquity was to believe and trust that Paladin's gift would save them … You and I must believe and trust in Jesus' gift to save us.

Chapter 4- Sin and Prayer

Choosing the right spiritual companion as you travel through life can make the difference between success and failure. This companion does not necessarily need to be a person. It could be a habit like sin or prayer. A travel companion who encourages you toward God will increase your chances of success. A travel companion who encourages you away from God will increase your chances of failure.

- As you read the story, take note of how the choices of travel companions made by the brothers affects their journey.

___

___

___

___

Chapter 5- Gerhorsam

Is participation in baptism an important step in a Christian's life?

Go therefore and make disciples of all the nations, baptizing them in the name of the Father and of the Son and of the Holy Spirit, teaching them to observe all things that I have commanded you;

and lo, I am with you always, even to the end of the age." Amen (Matt 28:19-20)

- What is baptism?

Therefore we were buried with Him through baptism into death, that just as Christ was raised from the dead by the glory of the Father, even so we also should walk in newness of life. (Rom 6:4)

- Would it be a good thing for you to be baptized? Should you be? Why or why not?

Chapter 6-Gravenwood

- What is an idol?

- What does God say about idols?

____

____

____

'You shall not make idols for yourselves; neither a carved image nor a sacred pillar shall you rear up for yourselves; nor shall you set up an engraved stone in your land, to bow down to it; for I am the Lord your God. (Leviticus 26:1)

Ponder points: A person, place or thing that has more of our devotion than God is an idol. Something to consider- How do you measure devotion? Perhaps you measure devotion by the amount of time and money that you spend on the attention of a person, place or thing.

____

____

____

- Do you have idols in your life? List them, and then put them in their proper place.

____

____

____

____

Chapter 7- Malevolence

"Enter by the narrow gate; for wide is the gate and broad is the way that leads to destruction, and there are many who go in by it. Because narrow is the gate and difficult is the way which leads to life, and there are few who find it. (Matthew 7:13,14)

There are only two basic paths you can take in life. Follow the world (i.e.-bad elements of pop culture; anything that goes against God's teaching) which is the broad road, or you might follow God's teaching, the narrow road.

- Name some examples of the broad road.

____

____

____

- Name some examples of the narrow road.

____

____

____

____

- As you read the story take note of how the boy's choices affect their lives.

____

____

____

____

- Which road are you on?

____

____

____

Chapter 8- Brawlers

- What is a bully?

____

____

____

- How should you react when confronted by a bully?

Ponder point: *A soft answer turns away wrath, But a harsh word stirs up anger. (Proverbs 15:1)*

____

____

____

- Should we respond with anger and rage? Why or why not.

____

____

____

- Should we respond with cool, calm and measured response? Why or why not?

____

____

____

____

- How did Jadan respond to the Brawler's threats?

____

____

____

____

- What was the consequence of Jadan's actions toward the Brawler's bullying?

____

____

____

____

Chapter 9- Badger Winds

- What is peer pressure?

- Is peer pressure good or bad? Why?

- What are some examples of good peer pressure?

- What are some examples of bad peer pressure?

- How is negative prejudice a fuel for bad peer pressure?

- What should our response be to bad peer pressure?

____

____

____

No temptation has overtaken you except such as is common to man; but God is faithful, who will not allow you to be tempted beyond what you are able, but with the temptation will also make the way of escape, that you may be able to bear it. (I Corinthians 10:13)

Chapter 10- The Keys

To become the kind of man God wants you to be you must possess a minimum of these four keys to manhood:

1. Vision
   - What is vision? Dream God's plan.

"Where there is no vision, the people perish." Proverbs 29:18 KJV (Authorized)

- Name some examples of how vision might look.

____

____

____

2. Courage
   - What is courage? Pursue your dream and never give up.

"Have I not commanded you? Be strong and of good courage; do not be afraid, nor be dismayed, for the LORD your God is with you wherever you go." Joshua 1:9

- List some examples of how courage should look.

___

___

___

3. Integrity
    - What is integrity? All your thoughts, words, and actions—God's way not yours.

"I know also, my God, that You test the heart and have pleasure in uprightness." I Chronicles 29:17

- List some examples of how integrity should look.

___

___

___

4. Service
    - What is service? (Use your personal resources to serve God and people.)

"'You shall love the LORD your God with all your heart, with all your soul, with all your strength, and with all your mind,' and "your neighbor as yourself."' Luke 10:27

- List some examples of how service might look.

Chapter 11- Mammon

...Lord, who may abide in Your tabernacle? Who may dwell in Your holy hill? He who walks uprightly, And works righteousness, And speaks the truth in his heart; He who does not backbite with his tongue, Nor does evil to his neighbor, Nor does he take up a reproach against his friend... (Psalms 15:1-3)

- What is a backbiter?

- How should you deal or respond to a backbiter? Why?

- List evidence of vision, courage, integrity or service found in Chapter 11- Mammon?

Chapter 12- Sea of Plethora

Ponder points: George Washington often quoted the French proverb: "[Gambling] is the child of avarice (greed), the brother of iniquity and the father of mischief." (Spinrad & Spinrad 1979). Thomas Jefferson said, "Gaming [gambling] corrupts our dispositions, and teaches us the habit of hostility against mankind." Benjamin Franklin, said in Poor Richard's Almanac, "Keep flax from fire, youth from gaming [gambling]."

- Is gambling immoral? Why or Why not?

- Is playing the lottery immoral? Why or why not?

- Is there harm in gambling?

- Are there dangers associated with gambling?

- List evidence of vision, courage, integrity or service found in Chapter 12- Sea of Plethora?

Chapter 13- The Fetter

The rich rules over the poor, And the borrower is servant to the lender. (Proverbs 22:7)

- When spending money, is it wise to spend more than you have? Why or why not.

- Is buying stuff on credit wise or unwise? Why or why not.

- Is using credit cards to buy possessions wise or unwise? Why or why not.

- How did Jerol deal with the Huckster's offer of a loan?

- List evidence of vision, courage, integrity or service found in Chapter 13- The Fetter?

Chapter 14- Coveton

"You shall not covet your neighbor's house; you shall not covet your neighbor's wife, nor his male servant, nor his female servant, nor his ox, nor his donkey, nor anything that is your neighbor's." (Exodus 20:17)

- What does coveting what belongs to someone else mean?

____

____

____

- How is coveting harmful?

____

____

____

- How did Jerol deal with the Covetons?

____

____

____

- List evidence of vision, courage, integrity or service found in Chapter 14- Coveton?

____

____

____

____

Chapter 15- Debt

But as he was not able to pay, his master commanded that he be sold, with his wife and children and all that he had, and that payment be made.(Matthew 18:25)

- What was the result of Jadan's use of the Fetter?

___

___

___

- Does the fetter remind you of a credit card? List how.

___

___

___

- List evidence of vision, courage, integrity or service found in Chapter 15- Debt?

___

___

___

Chapter 16- Euphoria & Chapter 17- The Lyrics

Do not let your adornment be merely outward--arranging the hair, wearing gold, or putting on fine apparel-- rather let it be the hidden person of the heart, with the incorruptible beauty of a gentle and quiet spirit, which is very precious in the sight of God. (I Peter 3:3,4)

- What do the clothes you wear say about you?

___

___

___

- Do the clothes you wear affect what people think about you? Why or why not.

___

___

___

- Does the kind of image you project around others really matter? Why or why not.

___

___

___

- Is having a tattoo wrong? Why or why not.

___

___

___

- Is having a body piercing wrong? Why or why not.

___

___

____

- Is body building wrong? Why or why not.

____

____

____

- List evidence of vision, courage, integrity or service found in Chapter 16- Euphoria & Chapter 17- The Lyrics?

____

____

____

Chapter 18- Bacchus

- Are drugs bad or good? Why or why not.

____

____

____

- What is the risk of abusing drugs?

____

____

____

- List evidence of vision, courage, integrity or service found in Chapter 18- Bacchus?

____

____

____

Chapter 19- Sunstones

And do not be conformed to this world, but be transformed by the renewing of your mind, that you may prove what is that good and acceptable and perfect will of God. (Romans 12:2)

- Is the content of today's media (T.V., radio, video games, commercials, etc.) good or bad? Why or why not.

____

____

____

Beloved, do not believe every spirit, but test the spirits, whether they are of God; because many false prophets have gone out into the world. (I John 4:1)

- What makes a song good or bad? The music? The lyric?

____

____

____

- Things to ask when exposed to today's media: Do the music, lyric, television program/commercial, or video game have a basis, and idea or purpose for its story?

  If so, might its basis, idea or purpose be traced back to an origin of light (God's way) or darkness (Evil's way)?

  Does the response you feel when viewing or listening to music, a lyric, a television program/commercial, or a video game, push you toward or away from what pleases God?

  Does how much time you spend daily watching T.V. or playing video games really matter? Why or why not.

____

____

____

- How does God want you to spend your time while here on earth? Does it matter? Why or why not.

____

____

____

____

- List evidence of vision, courage, integrity or service found in Chapter 19- Sunstones?

____

Chapter 20- Spirits

… do not be drunk with wine, in which is dissipation; but be filled with the Spirit, (Ephesians 5:18)

- How did Jadan approach Bacchus? What was the result?

- How did Jerol respond to peer pressure?

Blessed is the man who endures temptation; for when he has been approved, he will receive the crown of life which the Lord has promised to those who love Him. (James 1:12)

- How does God want us to respond when faced with peer pressure to try alcohol or drugs?

- List evidence of vision, courage, integrity or service found in Chapter 20- Spirits?

Chapter 21- Belle

Jerol received the key of service for his obedience to the Logos in defending Grace. By doing so he had displayed the highest level of concern for the protection of his fellow Terreneans. For turning away from the different temptations of Coveton and Euphoria he had been given the key of Integrity.

Read the following scriptures to get a better understanding of how God wants you to treat girls as well as guys.

Romans 12:5 and 13:8 and 15:7 & 14; Colossians 3:9 &13 & 16; I Corinthians 1:10 and 11:33 and 12:25 and 16:20; Romans 12:10 & 16 and 14:19 and 15:5 and 16:16; Hebrews 3:13 and 10:24 & 25 and 12:14; Ephesians 4:2 & 32 and 5:19 & 21; Galatians 5:13 and 6:2; I Peter 1:22 and 3:8 & 9 and 4:9 & 10 and 5: 5 & 14; I Thessalonians 4:18 and 5:11 & 14; Zechariah 7:9; James 5:16; I John 1:7; II Corinthians 13:12; John 13:34 & 35

- Put in your own words how God wants you to treat your fellowman. (girls and guys).

Read the following scripture to get a better understanding of how God does not want you to treat girls as well as guys.

Malachi 2:10; Romans 12:16 and 14:13; Galatians 5:26; Leviticus 19:11; I Peter 2:1 and 3:9 and 4:9; James 2:4 and 4:11

- Put in your own words how God does not want you to treat your fellowman. (girls and guys).

- How does God want a guy and a girl to treat one another before marriage?

- How does God want a guy and a girl to treat one another after marriage?

- Why did Jerol defend Grace against the Hellion?

___

___

___

- List evidence of vision, courage, integrity or service found in Chapter 21- Belle?

___

___

___

Chapter 22- Gevah

- List evidence of vision, courage, integrity or service found in Chapter 22- Gevah?

___

___

___

Chapter 23- Puffers & Chapter 24- Gascon

A man's pride will bring him low, But the humble in spirit will retain honor. (Proverbs 29:23)

- What is pride?

- Is pride good or bad? Why or why not?

Let nothing be done through selfish ambition or conceit, but in lowliness of mind let each esteem others better than himself.
(Phillipians 2:3)

- Is selfishness about being prideful? Why or why not?

- What is the affect on others when you focus too much attention on yourself?

- What happened to Jerol because of the Puffer's attention?

- How might unchecked selfishness lead to dangerous consequences?

- How might you guard your heart from being enslaved by pride?

- List evidence of vision, courage, integrity or service found in Chapter 23- Puffers & Chapter 24- Gascon?

Chapter 25- The Green River

Ponder points: Curiosity, alone, can lead to unhealthy revelations. Imagination, alone, can lead to unhealthy fantasies. Knowledge, alone, does not help anyone. Facts alone are only facts. Successfully solving life's problems requires a balance of curiosity, imagination, and knowledge filtered through the principles of God's Word.

- What are some examples of untamed curiosity? Untamed imagination? Untamed knowledge?

- What role might curiosity, imagination and knowledge play when making decisions and taking action?

- How do you filter your untamed curiosity, imagination and knowledge through God's word?

Ponder points: Don't let pride rob you of learning from someone else who has "been there and done that." Especially, heed the advice of experienced loved ones.

- List evidence of vision, courage, integrity or service found in Chapter 25- The Green River?

____

____

____

Chapter 26- The Bridge

So He said to them, "When you pray, say: Our Father in heaven, Hallowed be Your name. Your kingdom come. Your will be done On earth as it is in heaven. Give us day by day our daily bread. And forgive us our sins, For we also forgive everyone who is indebted to us. And do not lead us into temptation, But deliver us from the evil one." (Luke 11:2-4)

See Mark 6:5-13; Luke 11:9; Matthew 7:7-11; Matthew 26:39-42; I Timothy 2:1, Luke 18:1-8

- What is prayer?

____

____

____

____

- Is prayer to be used like a genie in a bottle?

- What is prayer's purpose?

- What interesting fact did Jerol learn about motives and Prayer? Do your motives have any impact on the results of your prayer?

- List evidence of vision, courage, integrity or service found in Chapter 26- The Bridge.

Chapter 27- Crossroad

...we also glory in tribulations, knowing that tribulation produces perseverance; and perseverance, character; and character, hope. Now hope does not disappoint, because the love of God has been poured out in our hearts by the Holy Spirit who was given to us. (Romans 5:3-5)

- What did Jerol do when faced with failure?

____

____

____

____

- What does perseverance mean?

____

____

____

____

- What does God say is the product of perseverance?

____

____

____

____

Ponder point: As long as you don't give up you can never be defeated.

- List evidence of vision, courage, integrity or service found in Chapter 27- The Crossroad.

____

____

____

____

Chapter 28- The Fording

- When all of Jerol's strength was gone what saved him?

____

____

____

- What lesson might we learn from Jerol's experience?

____

____

____

- List evidence of vision, courage, integrity or service found in Chapter 28- The Fording.

____

____

____

Chapter 29- The Door

... the sword of the Spirit, which is the Word of God ... (Ephesians 6:17)

- What offensive weapon did Jerol use to deal with Azrael?

____

____

____

- What weapon should we use to deal with the enemy in our daily life?

____

____

____

- List evidence of vision, courage, integrity or service found in Chapter 29- The Door.

____

____

____

____

Printed in the United States
125198LV00001B/209/A

9 780979 374401